LOVE IN VAIN

LOVE IN VAIN

Stories by LEWIS SHINER

Subterranean Press • 2001

FIRST EDITION
Spetember 2001

ISBN 1-931081-15-8

Subteranean Presss
P.O. Box 190106
Burton, MI 48519

email:
publisher@subterraneanpress.com

website:
www.subterraneanpress.com

TABLE OF CONTENTS

I'd like to send a big thank you to gentleman editor Bill Schafer, who finally made this book a reality, along with special thanks to cover artist and designer Gail Cross, who outdid herself for me. Thanks also to the editors who first published these stories: Lou Aronica, Ellen Datlow, Gardner Dozois, Lucinda Ebersole, Jeff Goodman, Anne Jordan, Steve Kane, Chris Kelly, Joe Lansdale, Karen Lansdale, Pat LoBrutto, Shawna McCarthy, Richard Peabody, Lee Schultz, Andy Watson, Sheila Williams, J. Peder Zane, and Mark Ziesing.

LOVE IN VAIN

For James Ellroy

THE ROOM had whitewashed walls, no windows, and a map of the US on my left as I came in. There must have been a hundred pins with little colored heads stuck along the interstates. By the other door was a wooden table, the top full of scratches and coffee rings. Charlie was already sitting on the far side of it.

They called it Charlie's "office" and a Texas Ranger named Gonzales had brought me back there to meet him. "Charlie?" Gonzales said. "This here's Dave McKenna. He's an Assistant D.A. up in Dallas?"

"Morning," Charlie said. His left eye, the glass one, drooped a little, and his teeth were brown and ragged. He had on jeans and a plaid short-sleeved shirt and he was shaved clean. His hair was damp and combed straight back. His sideburns had gray in them and came to the bottom of his ears.

I had files and a notebook in my right hand so I wouldn't have to shake with him. He didn't offer. "You looking to close you up some cases?" he said.

I had to clear my throat. "Well, we thought we might give it a try." I sat down in the other chair.

He nodded and looked at Gonzales. "Ernie? You don't suppose I could have a little more coffee?"

Gonzales had been leaning against the wall by the map, but he straightened right up and said, "Sure thing, Charlie." He brought in a full pot from the other room and set it on the table. Charlie had a styrofoam cup that held about a quart. He filled it up and then added three packets of sugar and some powdered creamer.

"How about you?" Charlie said.

"No," I said. "Thanks."

"You don't need to be nervous," Charlie said. His breath smelled of coffee and cigarettes. When he wasn't talking his mouth relaxed into an easy smile. You didn't have to see anything menacing in it. It was the kind of smile you could see from any highway in Texas, looking out at you from a porch or behind a gas pump, waiting for you to drive on through.

I took out a little pocket-sized cassette recorder. "Would it be okay if I taped this?"

"Sure, go ahead."

I pushed the little orange button on top. "March 27, Williamson County Jail. Present are Sergeant Ernesto Gonzales and Charles Dean Harris."

"Charlie," he said.

"Pardon?"

"Nobody ever calls me Charles."

"Right," I said. "Okay."

"I guess maybe my mother did sometimes. Always sounded wrong somehow." He tilted his chair back against the wall. "You don't suppose you could back that up and do it over?"

"Yeah, okay, fine." I rewound the tape and went through the introduction again. This time I called him Charlie.

Twenty-five years ago he'd stabbed his mother to death. She'd been his first.

IT HAD TAKEN ME three hours to drive from Dallas to the Williamson County Jail in Georgetown, a straight shot down Interstate 35. I'd left a little before eight that morning. Alice was already at work and I had to get Jeffrey off to school. The hardest part was getting him away from the television.

He was watching MTV. They were playing the Heart video where the blonde guitar player wears the low-cut golden prom dress. Every time she moved her magnificent breasts seemed to hesitate before they went along, like they were proud, willful animals, just barely under her control.

I turned the TV off and swung Jeffrey around a couple of times and sent him out for the bus. I got together the files I needed and went into the bedroom to make the bed. The covers were turned back on both sides, but the middle was undisturbed. Alice and I hadn't made love in six weeks. And counting.

I walked through the house, picking up Jeffrey's Masters of the Universe toys. I saw that Alice had loaded up the mantel again with framed pictures of her brothers and parents and the dog she'd had as a little girl. For a second it seemed like the entire house was buried in objects that had nothing to do with me—dolls and vases and doilies and candles and baskets on every inch of every flat surface she could reach. You couldn't walk from one end of a room to the other without running into a Victorian chair or secretary or umbrella stand, couldn't see the floors for the flowered rugs.

I locked up and got in the car and took the LBJ loop all the way around town. The idea was to avoid traffic. I was kidding myself. Driving in Dallas is a matter of manly pride: if somebody manages to pull in front of you he's clearly got a bigger dick than you do. Rather than let this happen it's better that one of you die.

I was in traffic the whole way down, through a hundred and seventy miles of Charlie Dean Harris country: flat, desolate grasslands with an occasional bridge or culvert where you could dump a body. Charlie had wandered and murdered all over the south, but once he found I-35 he was home to stay.

I OPENED ONE of the folders and rested it against the edge of the table so Charlie wouldn't see my hand tremble. "I've got a case here from 1974. A Dallas girl on her way home from Austin for spring break. Her name was Carol, uh, Fairchild. Black hair, blue eyes. Eighteen years old."

Charlie was nodding. "She had braces on her teeth. Would have been real pretty without 'em."

I looked at the sheet of paper in the folder. Braces, it said. The plain white walls seemed to wobble a little. "Then you remember her."

"Yessir, I suppose I do. I killed her." He smiled. It looked like a reflex, something he didn't even know he was doing. "I killed her to have sex with her."

"Can you remember anything else?"

He shrugged. "It was just to have sex, that's all. I remember when she got in the car. She was wearing a T-shirt, one of them man's T-shirts, with the straps and all." He dropped the chair back down and put his elbows on the table. "You could see her titties," he explained.

I wanted to pull away but I didn't. "Where was this?"

He thought for a minute. "Between here and Round Rock, right there off the Interstate."

I looked down at my folder again. Last seen wearing navy tank top, blue jeans. "What color was the T-shirt?"

"Red," he said. "She would have been strangled. With a piece of electrical wire I had there in the car. I had supposed she was a prostitute, dressed the way she was and all. I asked her to have sex and she said she would, so I got off the highway and then she didn't want to. So I killed her and I had sex with her."

Nobody said anything for what must have been at least a minute. I could hear a little scratching noise as the tape moved inside the recorder. Charlie was looking straight at me with his good eye. "I wasn't satisfied," he said.

"What?"

"I wasn't satisfied. I had sex with her but I wasn't satisfied."

"Listen, you don't have to tell me..."

"I got to tell it all," he said.

"I don't want to hear it," I said. My voice came out too high, too loud. But Charlie kept staring at me.

"It don't matter," he said. "I still got to tell it. I got to tell it all. I can't live with the terrible things I did. Jesus says that if I tell everything I can be with Betsy when this is all over." Betsy was his common law wife. He'd killed her too, after living with her since she was nine. The words sounded like he'd practiced them, over and over.

"I'll take you to her if you want," he said.

"Betsy...?"

"No, your girl there. Carol Fairchild. I'll take you where I buried her." He wasn't smiling any more. He had the sad, earnest look of a laundromat bum telling you how he'd lost his oil fortune up in Oklahoma.

I looked at Gonzales. "We can set it up for you if you want," he said. "Sheriff'll have to okay it and all, but we could prob'ly do it first thing tomorrow."

"Okay," I said. "That'd be good."

Charlie nodded, drank some coffee, lit a cigarette. "Well, fine," he said. "You want to try another?"

"No," I said. "Not just yet."

"Whatever," Charlie said. "You just let me know."

Later, walking me out, Gonzales said, "Don't let Charlie get to you. He wants people to like him, you know? So he figures out what you want him to be, and he tries to be that for you."

I knew he was trying to cheer me up. I thanked him and told him I'd be back in the morning.

I CALLED ALICE from my friend Jack's office in Austin, thirty miles farther down I-35. "It's me," I said.

"Oh," she said. She sounded tired. "How's it going?"

I didn't know what to tell her. "Fine," I said. "I need to stay over another day or so."

"Okay," she said.

"Are you okay?"

"Fine," she said.

"Jeffrey?"

"He's fine."

I watched thirty seconds tick by on Jack's wall clock. "Anything else?" she said.

"I guess not." My eyes stung and I reflexively shaded them with my free hand. "I'll be at Jack's if you need me."

"Okay," she said. I waited a while longer and then put the phone back on the hook.

Jack had just come out of his office. "Oh oh," he said.

It took a couple of breaths to get my throat to unclench. "Yeah," I said.

"Bad?"

"Bad as it could be, I guess. It's over, probably. I mean, I think it's over, but how do you know?"

"You don't," Jack said. His secretary, a good-looking Chicana named Liz, typed away on her word processor and tried to act like she wasn't having to listen to us. "You just after a while get fed up and you say fuck it. You want to get a burger or what?"

JACK AND I went to UT law school together. He'd lost a lot of hair and put on some weight but he wouldn't do anything about it. Jogging was for assholes. He would rather die fat and keep his self-respect.

He'd been divorced two years now and was always glad to fold out the couch for me. It had been a while. After Jeffrey was born Alice and I had somehow lost touch with everything except work and TV. "I've missed this," I said.

"Missed what?"

"Friends," I said. We were in a big prairie-style house north of campus that had been fixed up with a kitchen and bar and hanging plants. I was full, but still working on the last of the batter-dipped french fries.

"Not my fault, you prick. You're the one dropped down to Christmas cards."

"Yeah, well…"

"Forget it. How'd it go with Charlie Dean?"

"Unbelievable," I said. "I mean, really. He confessed to everything. Had details. Even had a couple wrong, enough to look good. But the major stuff was right on."

"So that's great. Isn't it?"

"It was a set up. The name I gave him was a fake. No such person, no such case."

"I don't get it."

"Jack, the son of a bitch has confessed to something like three thousand murders. It ain't possible. So they wanted to catch him lying."

"With his pants down, so to speak."

"Same old Jack."

"You said he had details."

"That's the creepy part. He knew she was supposed to have braces. I had it in the phoney case file, but he brought it up before I did."

"Lucky guess."

"No. It was too creepy. And there's all this shit he keeps telling you. Things you wish you'd never heard, you know what I mean?"

"I know exactly what you mean," Jack said. "When I was in junior high I saw a bum go in the men's room at the bus station with a loaf of bread. I told this friend of mine about it and he says the bum was going in there to wipe all the dried piss off the toilets with the bread and then eat it. For the protein. Said it happens all the time."

"Jesus Christ, Jack."

"See? I know what you're talking about. There's things you don't want in your head. Once they get in there, you're not the same any more. I can't eat white bread to this day. Twenty years, and I still can't touch it."

"You asshole." I pushed my plate away and finished my Corona. "Christ, now the beer tastes like piss."

Jack pointed his index finger at me. "You will never be the same," he said.

YOU COULD NEVER TELL how much Jack had been drinking. He said it was because he was careful not to let on if he was ever sober. I always thought it was because there was something in him that was meaner than the booze and together they left him just about even.

It was a lot of beers later that Jack said, "What was the name of that bimbo in high school you used to talk about? Your first great love or some shit? Except she never put out for you?"

"Kristi," I said. "Kristi Spector."

"Right!" Jack got up and started to walk around the apartment. It wasn't too long of a walk. "A name like that, how could I forget? I got her off a soliciting rap two months ago."

"Soliciting?"

"There's a law in Texas against selling your pussy. Maybe you didn't know that."

"Kristi Spector, my god. Tell me about it."

"She's a stripper, son. Works over at the Yellow Rose. This guy figured if she'd show her tits in public he could have the rest in his car. She didn't, he called the pigs. Said she made lewd advances. Crock of shit, got thrown out of court."

"How's she look?"

"Not too goddamn bad. I wouldn't have minded taking my fee in trade, but she didn't seem to get the hint." He stopped. "I got a better idea. Let's go have a look for ourselves."

"Oh no," I said.

"Oh yes. She remembers you, man. She says you were 'sweet.' Come on, get up. We're going to go look at some tits."

THE PLACE was bigger inside than I expected, the ceilings higher. There were two stages and a runway behind the second one. There were stools right up by the stages for the guys that wanted to stick dollar bills in the dancers' G-strings and four-top tables everywhere else.

I should have felt guilty but I wasn't thinking about Alice at all. The issue here was sex, and Alice had written herself out of that part of my life. Instead I was thinking about the last time I'd seen Kristi.

It was senior year in high school. The director of the drama club, who was from New York, had invited some of us to a "wild" party. It was the first time I'd seen men in dresses. I'd locked myself in the bathroom with Kristi to help her take her bra off. I hadn't seen her in six months. She'd just had an abortion; the father could have been one of a couple of guys. Not me. She didn't want to spoil what we had. It was starting to look to me like there wasn't much left to spoil. That had been 18 years ago.

The DJ played something by Pat Benatar. The music was loud enough to give you a kind of mental privacy. You didn't really have to pay attention to anything but the dancers. At the moment it seemed like just the thing. It had been an ugly day and there was something in me that was comforted by the sight of young, good looking women with their clothes off.

"College town," Jack said, leaning toward me so I could hear him. "Lots of local talent."

A tall blonde on the north stage unbuttoned her long-sleeved white shirt and let it hang open. Her breasts were smooth and firm and pale. Like the others she had something on the point of her nipples that made a small, golden flash every time one caught the light.

"See anybody you know?"

"Give me a break," I shouted over the music. "You saw her a couple months ago. It's been almost twenty years for me. I may not even recognize her." A waitress came by, wearing black leather jeans and a red tank top. For a second I could hear Charlie's voice telling me about her titties. I rubbed the sides of my head and the voice went away. We ordered beers, but when they came my stomach was wrapped around itself and I had to let mine sit.

"It's got to be weird to do this for a living," I said in Jack's ear.

"Bullshit," Jack said. "You think they're not getting off on it?"

He pointed to the south stage. A brunette in high heels had let an overweight man in sideburns and a western shirt tuck a dollar into the side of her bikini bottoms. He talked earnestly to her with just the start of an embarrassed smile. She had to keep leaning closer to hear him. Finally she nodded and turned around. She bent over and grabbed her ankles. His face was about the height of the backs of her knees. She was smiling like she'd just seen somebody else's baby do something cute. After a few seconds she stood up again and the man went back to his table.

"What was that about?" I asked Jack.

"Power, man," he said. "God, I love women. I just love 'em."

"Your problem is you don't know the difference between love and sex."

"Yeah? What is it? Come on, I want to know." The music was too loud to argue with him. I shook my head. "See? You don't know either."

The brunette pushed her hair back with both hands, chin up, fingers spread wide, and it reminded me of Kristi. The theatricality of it. She'd played one of Tennessee Williams' affected Southern bitches once and it had been almost too painful to watch. Almost.

"Come on," I said, grabbing Jack's sleeve. "It's been swell, but let's get out of here. I don't need to see her. I'm better off with the fantasy."

Jack didn't say anything. He just pointed with his chin to the stage behind me.

She had on a leopard skin leotard. She had been a dark blonde in high school but now her hair was brown and short. She'd put on a little weight, not much. She stretched in front of the mirrored wall and the DJ played the Pretenders.

I felt this weird, possessive kind of pride, watching her. That and lust. I'd been married for eight years and the worst thing I'd ever done was kiss an old girl friend on New Year's Eve and stare longingly at the pictures in *Playboy*. But this was real, this was happening.

The song finished and another one started and she pulled one strap down on the leotard. I remembered the first time I'd seen her breasts. I was fifteen. I'd joined a youth club at the Unitarian Church because she went there Sunday afternoons. Sometimes we would skip the program and sneak off into the deserted Sunday school classrooms and there, in the twilight, surrounded by crayon drawings on manila paper, she would stretch out on the linoleum and let me lie on top of her and feel the maddening pressure of her pelvis and smell the faint, clinically erotic odor of peroxide in her hair.

She showed me her breasts on the golf course next door. We had jumped the fence and we lay in a sandtrap so no one would see us. There was a little light from the street, but not enough for real color. It was like a black and white movie when I played it back in my mind.

They were fuller now, hung a little lower and flatter, but I remembered the small, pale nipples. She pulled the other strap down, turned her back, rotating her hips as she stripped down to a red G-string. Somebody held a dollar out to her. I wanted to go over there and tell him that I knew her.

Jack kept poking me in the ribs. "Well? Well?"

"Be cool," I said. I had been watching the traffic pattern and I knew that after the song she would take a break and then get up on the other stage. It took a long time, but I wasn't tense about it. I'm just going to say hi, I thought. And that's it.

The song was over and she walked down the stairs at the end of the stage, throwing the leotard around her shoulders. I got up, having a little trouble with the chair, and walked over to her.

"Kristi," I said. "It's Dave McKenna."

"Oh my God!" She was in my arms. Her skin was hot from the lights and I could smell her deodorant. I was suddenly dizzy, aware of every square inch where our bodies touched. "Do you still hate me?" she said as she pulled away.

"What?" There was so much I'd forgotten. The twang in her voice. The milk chocolate color of her eyes. The beauty mark over her right cheekbone. The flirtatious look up through the lashes that now had a desperate edge to it.

"The last time I saw you, you called me a bitch. It was after that party at your teacher's house."

"No, I...believe me, it wasn't like..."

"Listen, I'm on again," she said. "Where are you?"

"We're right over there."

"Oh Christ, you didn't bring your wife with you? I heard you were married."

"No, it's..."

"I got to run, sugar, wait for me."

I went back to the table.

"You rascal," Jack said. "Why didn't you just slip it to her on the spot?"

"Shut up, Jack, will you?"

"Ooooh, touchy."

I watched her dance. She was no movie star. Her face was a little hard and even the heavy makeup didn't hide all the lines. But none of that mattered. What mattered was the way she moved, the kind of puckered smile that said yes, I want it too.

SHE SAT DOWN with us when she was finished. She seemed to be all hands, touching me on the arm, biting on a fingernail, gesturing in front of her face.

She was dancing three times a week, which was all they would schedule her for any more. The money was good and she didn't mind the work, especially here where it wasn't too rowdy. Jack raised his eyebrows at me to say, see? She got by with some modeling and some "scuffling" which I assumed meant turning tricks. Her mother was still in Dallas and had sent Kristi clippings the couple of times I got my name in the paper.

"She always liked me," I said.

"She liked you the best of all of them. You were a gentleman."

"Maybe too much of one."

"It was why I loved you." She was wearing the leotard again but she might as well have been naked. I was beginning to be afraid of her so I reminded myself that nothing had happened yet, nothing had to happen, that I wasn't committed to anything. I pushed my beer over to her and she drank about half of it. "It gets hot up there," she said. "You wouldn't believe. Sometimes you think you're going to pass out, but you got to keep smiling."

"Are you married?" I asked her. "Were you ever?"

"Once. It lasted two whole months. The shitheel knocked me up and then split."

"What happened?"

"I kept the kid. He's four now."

"What's his name?"

"Stoney. He's a cute little bastard. I got a neighbor watches him when I'm out, and I do the same for hers. He keeps me going sometimes." She drank the rest of the beer. "What about you?"

"I got a little boy too. Jeffrey. He's seven."

"Just the one?"

"I don't think the marriage could handle more than one kid," I said.

"It's an old story," Jack said. "If your wife puts you through law school, the marriage breaks up. It just took Dave a little longer than most."

"You're getting divorced?" she asked.

"I don't know. Maybe." She nodded. I guess she didn't need to ask for details. Marriages come apart every day.

"I'm on again in a little," she said. "Will you still be here when I get back?" She did what she could to make it sound casual.

"I got an early day tomorrow," I said.

"Sure. It was good to see you. Real good."

The easiest thing seemed to be to get out a pen and an old business card. "Give me your phone number. Maybe I can get loose another night."

She took the pen but she kept looking at me. "Sure," she said.

"YOU'RE AN IDIOT," Jack said. "Why didn't you go home with her?"

I watched the streetlights. My jacket smelled like cigarettes and my head had started to hurt.

"That gorgeous piece of ass says to you, 'Ecstasy?' and Dave says, 'No thanks.' What the hell's the matter with you? Alice make you leave your dick in the safe deposit box?"

"Jack," I said, "will you shut the fuck up?" The card with her number on it was in the inside pocket of the jacket. I could feel it there, like a cool fingernail against my flesh.

JACK WENT BACK to his room to crash a little after midnight. I couldn't sleep. I put on the headphones and listened to Robert Johnson, "King of the Delta Blues Singers." There was something about his voice. He had this deadpan tone that sat down and told you what was wrong like it was no big deal. Then the voice would crack and you could tell it was a hell of a lot worse than he was letting on.

They said the devil himself had tuned Johnson's guitar. He died in 1938, poisoned by jealous husband. He'd made his first recordings in a hotel room in San Antonio, just another 70 miles on down I-35.

CHARLIE AND GONZALES and I took my car out to what Gonzales called the "site." The sheriff and a deputy were in a brown county station wagon behind us. Charlie sat on the passenger side and Gonzales was in the back. Charlie could have opened the door at a stoplight and been gone. He wasn't even in handcuffs. Nobody said anything about it.

We got on I-35 and Charlie said, "Go on south to the second exit after the caves." The Inner Space Caverns were just south of Georgetown, basically a single long, unspectacular tunnel that ran for miles under the highway. "I killed a girl there once. When they turned off the lights."

I nodded but I didn't say anything. That morning, before I went in to the "office," Gonzales had told me that it made Charlie angry if you let on that you didn't believe him. I was tired, and hungover from watching Jack drink, and I didn't really give a damn about Charlie's feelings.

I got off at the exit and followed the access road for a while. Charlie had his eyes closed and seemed to be thinking hard.

"Having trouble?" I asked him.

"Nah," he said. "Just didn't want to take you to the wrong one." I looked at him and he started laughing. It was a joke. Gonzales chuckled in the back seat and there was this cheerful kind of feeling in the car that made me want to pull over and run away.

"Nosir," Charlie said, "I sure don't suppose I'd want to do that." He grinned at me and he knew what I was thinking, he could see the horror right there on my face. He just kept smiling. Come on, I could hear him say. Loosen up. Be one of the guys.

I wiped the sweat from my hands onto my pant legs. Finally he said, "There's a dirt road a ways ahead. Turn off on it. It'll go over a hill and then across a cattle grating. After the grating is a stand of trees to the left. You'll want to park up under 'em."

How can he do this? I thought. He's got to know there's nothing there. Or does he? When we don't turn anything up, what's he going to do? Are they going to wish they'd cuffed him after all? The sheriff knew what I was up to, but none of the others did. Would Gonzales turn on me for betraying Charlie?

The road did just what Charlie said it would. We parked the cars under the trees and the deputy and I got shovels out of the sheriff's trunk. The trees were oaks and their leaves were tiny and very pale green.

"It would be over here," Charlie said. He stood on a patch of low ground, covered with clumps of Johnson grass. "Not too deep."

He was right. She was only about six or eight inches down. The deputy had a body bag and he tried to move her into it, but she kept coming apart. There wasn't much left but a skeleton and a few rags.

And the braces. Still shining, clinging to the teeth of the skull like a metal smile.

ON THE WAY BACK to Georgetown we passed a woman on the side of the road. She was staring into the hood of her car. She looked like she was about to cry. Charlie turned all the way around in his seat to watch her as we drove by.

"There's just victims ever'where," Charlie said. There was a sadness in his voice I didn't believe. "The highway's full of 'em. Kids, hitchhikers, waitresses…You ever pick one up?"

"No," I said, but it wasn't true. It was in Dallas, I was home for spring break. It was the end of the sixties. She had on a green dress. Nothing happened. But she had smiled at me and put one arm up on the back of the seat. I was on the way to my girlfriend's house and I let her off a few blocks away. And that night, when I was inside her, I imagined my girlfriend with the hitchhiker's face, with her blonde hair and freckles, her slightly coarse features, the dots of sweat on her upper lip.

"But you thought about it," Charlie said. "Didn't you?"

"Listen," I said. "I've got a job to do. I just want to do it and get out of here, okay?"

"I know what you're saying," Charlie said. "Jesus forgives me, but I can't ask that of nobody else. I was just trying to get along, that's all. That's all any of us is ever trying to do."

I CALLED DALLAS collect from the sheriff's phone. He gave me a private room where I could shout if I had to. The switchboard put me through to Ricky Slatkin, Senior Assistant D.A. for Homicide.

"Dave, will you for Chrissake calm down. It's a coincidence. That's all. Forensics will figure out who this girl is and we'll put another 70 or 80 years on Charlie's sentence. Maybe give him another death penalty. What the hell, right? Meanwhile we'll give him another ringer."

"You give him one. I want out of this. I am fucking terrified."

"I, uh, understand you're under some stress at home these days."

"I am not at home. I'm in Georgetown, in the Williamson County Jail, and I am under some fucking stress right here. Don't you understand? He thought this dead girl into existence."

"What, Charlie Dean Harris is God now, is that it? Come on, Dave. Go out and have a few beers and by tomorrow it'll all make sense to you."

"HE'S EVIL, JACK," I said. We were back at his place after a pizza at Conan's. Jack had ordered a pitcher of beer and drunk it all himself. "I didn't use to believe in it, but that was before I met Charlie."

He had a women's basketball game on TV, the sound turned down to a low hum. "That's horseshit," he said. His voice was too loud. "Horseshit, Christian horseshit. They want you to believe that Evil has got a capital E and it's sitting over there in the corner, see it? Horseshit. Evil isn't a thing. It's something that's not there. It's an absence. The lack of the thing that stops you from doing whatever you damn well please."

He chugged half a beer. "Your pal Charlie ain't evil. He's just damaged goods. He's just like you or me but something died in him. You know what I'm talking about. You've felt it. First it goes to sleep and then it dies. Like when you stand up in court and try to get a rapist off when you know he did it. You tell yourself that it's part of the game, you try to give the asshole the benefit of the doubt, hell, somebody's got to do it, right? You try to believe the girl is just some slut that changed her mind, but you can smell it. Something inside you starting to rot."

He finished the beer and threw it at a paper sack in the corner. It hit another bottle inside the sack and shattered. "Then you go home and your wife's got a goddamn headache or her period or she's asleep in front of the TV or she's not in the goddamn mood and you just want to beat the..." His right fist was clenched up so tight the knuckles were a shiny yellow. His eyes looked like open sores. He got up for another beer and he was in the kitchen for a long time.

When he came back I said, "I'm going out." I said it without giving myself a chance to think about it.

"Kristi," Jack said. He had a fresh beer and was all right again. "Yeah."

"You bastard! Can I smell your fingers when you get back?"

"Fuck you, Jack."

"Oh no, save it for her. She's going to use you up, you lucky bastard."

I CALLED HER from a pay phone and she gave me directions. She was at the Royal Palms Trailer Park, near Bergstrom Air Force Base on the south end of town. It wasn't hard to find. They even had a few palm trees. There were rural-type galvanized mailboxes on posts by the gravel driveways. I found the one that said Spector and parked behind a white Dodge with six-figure mileage.

The temperature was in the sixties but I was shaking. My shoulders kept trying to crawl up around my neck. I got out of the car. I couldn't feel my feet. Asshole, I told myself. I don't want to hear about your personal problems. You better enjoy this or I'll fucking kill you.

I knocked on the door and it made a kind of mute rattling sound. Kristi opened it. She was wearing a plaid bathrobe, so old I couldn't tell what the colors used to be. She stood back to let me in and said, "I didn't think you'd call."

"But I did," I said. The trailer was tiny—a living room with a green sofa and a 13-inch color TV, a kitchen the size of a short hall, a single bedroom behind it, the door open, the bed unmade. A blond-haired boy was asleep on the sofa, wrapped in an army blanket. The shelf above him was full of plays—Albee, Ionesco, Tennessee Williams. The walls were covered with photographs in dime-store frames.

A couple of them were from the drama club; one even had me in it. I was sixteen and looked maybe nine. My hair was too long in front, my chest was sucked in, and I had a stupid smirk on my face. I was looking at Kristi. Who would want to look at anything else? She had on cutoffs that had frayed up past the crease of her thighs. Her shirt was unbuttoned and tied under her breasts. Her head was back and she was laughing. I'd always been able to make her laugh.

"You want a drink?" she whispered.

"No," I said. I turned to look at her. We weren't either of us laughing now. I reached for her and she glanced over at the boy and shook her head. She grabbed the cuff of my shirt and pulled me gently back toward the bedroom.

It smelled of perfume and hand lotion and a little of mildew. The only light trickled in through heavy, old-fashioned venetian blinds. She untied the bathrobe and let it fall. I kissed her and her arms went around my neck. I touched her shoulder blades and her hair and her buttocks and then I got out of my clothes and left them in a pile on the floor. She ran on tiptoes back to the front of the trailer and locked and chained the door. Then she came back and shut the bedroom door and lay down on the bed.

I lay down next to her. The smell and feel of her was wonderful, and at the same time it was not quite real. There were too many unfamiliar things and it was hard to connect to the rest of my life.

Then I was on my knees between her legs, gently touching her. Her arms were spread out beside her, tangled in the sheets, her hips moving with pleasure. Only once, in high school, had she let me touch her there, in the back seat of a friend's car, her skirt up around her hips, panties to her knees, and before I had recovered from the wonder of it she had pulled away.

But that was 18 years ago and this was now. A lot of men had touched her since then. But that was all right. She took a condom out of the nightstand and I put it on and she guided me inside her. She tried to say something, maybe it was only my name, but I put my mouth over hers to shut her up. I put both my arms around her and closed my eyes and let the heat and pleasure run up through me.

When I finished and we rolled apart she lay on top of me, pinning me to the bed. "That was real sweet," she said.

I kissed her and hugged her because I couldn't say what I was thinking. I was thinking about Charlie, remembering the earnest look on his face when he said, "It was just to have sex, that's all."

SHE WAS WIDE AWAKE and I was exhausted. She complained about the state cutting back on aid to single parents. She told me about the tiny pieces of tape she had to wear on the ends of her nipples when she danced, a weird Health Department regulation. I remembered the tiny golden flashes and fell asleep to the memory of her dancing.

Screaming woke me up. Kristi was already out of bed and headed for the living room. "It's just Stoney," she said, and I lay back down.

I woke up again a little before dawn. There was an arm around my waist but it seemed much too small. I rolled over and saw that the little boy had crawled into bed between us.

I got up without moving him and went to the bathroom. There was no water in the toilet; when I pushed the handle a trap opened in the bottom of the bowl and a fine spray washed the sides. I got dressed, trying not to bump into anything. Kristi was asleep on the side of the bed closest to the door, her mouth open a little. Stoney had burrowed into the middle of her back.

I was going to turn around and go when a voyeuristic impulse made me open the drawer of her nightstand. Or maybe I subconsciously knew what I'd find. There was a Beeline book called *Molly's Sexual Follies,* a tube of KY, a box of Ramses lubricated condoms, a few used Kleenex. An emery board, a finger puppet, one hoop earring. A short barreled Colt .32 revolver.

I GOT TO THE JAIL at nine in the morning. The woman at the visitor's window recognized me and buzzed me back. Gonzales was at his desk. He looked up when I walked in and said, "I didn't know you was coming in today."

"I just had a couple of quick questions for Charlie," I said. "Only take a second."

"Did you want to use the office…?"

"No, no point. If I could just talk to him in his cell for a couple of minutes, that would be great."

Gonzales got the keys. Charlie had a cell to himself, five by ten feet, white-painted bars on the long wall facing the corridor. There were Bibles and religious tracts on his cot, a few paintings hanging on the wall. "Maybe you can get Charlie to show you his pictures," Gonzales said. A stool in the corner had brushes and tubes of paint on the top.

"You painted these?" I asked Charlie. My voice sounded fairly normal, all things considered.

"Yessir, I did."

"They're pretty good." They were landscapes with trees and horses, but no people.

"Thank you kindly."

"You can just call for me when you're ready," Gonzales said. He went out and locked the door.

"I thought you'd be back," Charlie said. "Was there something else you wanted to ask me?" He sat on the edge of the cot, forearms on his knees.

I didn't say anything. I took the Colt out of the waistband of my pants and pointed it at him. I'd already looked it over on the drive up and there were bullets in all six cylinders. My hand was shaking so I steadied it with my left and fired all six rounds into his head and chest.

I hadn't noticed all the background noises until they stopped, the typewriters and the birds and somebody singing upstairs. Charlie stood up and walked over to where I was standing. The revolver clicked on an empty shell.

"You can't kill me," Charlie said with his droopy-eyed smile. "You can't never kill me." The door banged open at the end of the hall. "You can't kill me because I'm inside you."

I dropped the gun and locked my hands behind my head. Gonzales stuck his head around the corner. He was squinting. He had his gun out and he looked terrified. Charlie and I stared back at him calmly.

"It's okay, Ernie," Charlie said. "No harm done. Mr. McKenna was just having him a little joke."

CHARLIE TOLD GONZALES the gun was loaded with blanks. They had to believe him because there weren't any bulletholes in the cell. I told them I'd bought the gun off a defendant years ago, that I'd had it in the car.

They called Dallas and Ricky asked to talk to me. "There's going to be an inquiry," he said. "No way around it."

"Sure there is," I said. "I quit. I'll send it to you in writing. I'll put it in the mail today. Express."

"You need some help, Dave. You understand what I'm saying to you here? Professional help. Think about it. Just tell me you'll think about it."

Gonzales was scared and angry and wanted me charged with smuggling weapons into the jail. The sheriff knew it wasn't worth the headlines and by suppertime I was out.

Jack had already heard about it through some kind of legal grapevine. He thought it was funny. We skipped dinner and went down to the bars on Sixth Street. I couldn't drink anything. I was afraid of going numb, or letting down my guard. But Jack made up for me. As usual.

"Kristi called me today," Jack said. "I told her I didn't know but what you might be going back to Dallas today. Just a kind of feeling I had."

"I'm not going back," I said. "But it was the right thing to tell her."

"Not what it was cracked up to be, huh?"

"Oh yeah," I said. "That and much, much more."

For once he let it go. "You mean you're not going back tonight or not going back period?"

"Period," I said. "My job's gone, I pissed that away this morning. I'll get something down here. I don't care what. I'll pump gas. I'll fucking wait tables. You can draw up the divorce papers and I'll sign them."

"Just like that?"

"Just like that."

"What's Alice going to say?"

"I don't know if she'll even notice. She can have the goddamn house and her car and the savings. All of it. All I want is some time with Jeffrey. As much as I can get. Every week if I can."

"Good luck."

"I've got to have it. I don't want him growing up screwed up like the rest of us. I've got stuff I've got to tell him. He's going to need help. All of us are. Jack, goddamn it, are you listening to me?"

He wasn't. He was staring at the Heart video on the bar's big screen TV, at the blonde guitarist. "Look at that," Jack said. "Sweet suffering Jesus. Couldn't you just fuck that to death?"

His Girlfriend's Dog

ONE DAY he saw himself the way his girlfriend's dog saw him. Huge, slow, precariously built, insensitive to moods and hungers and smells, overly fastidious about privates and dung. Soon he found his girlfriend incomprehensible, perhaps even cruel. Her actions seemed deliberately meant to puzzle him. His sense of play offended her.

After they broke up she would call him. "Ernie misses you," she would say.

"What about you?"

"Of course not," she would say, confusing him yet again. "He sees me every day."

WHITE CITY

TESLA LIFTS the piece of sirloin to his lips. Its volume is approximately .25 cubic inches, or .02777 of the entire steak. As he chews, he notices a waterspot on the back of his fork. He takes a fresh napkin from the stack at his left elbow and scrubs the fork vigorously.

He is sitting at a private table in the refreshment stand at the west end of the Court of Honor. He looks out onto the Chicago World's Fair and Columbian Exposition. It is October of 1893. The sun is long gone and the reflections of Tesla's electric lights sparkle on the surface of the Main Basin, turning the spray from the fountain into glittering jewels. At the far end of the Basin stands the olive-wreathed Statue of the Republic in flowing robes. On all sides the White City lies in pristine elegance, testimony to the glorious architecture of ancient Greece and Rome. Its chilly streets are populated by mustached men in topcoats and sturdy women in woolen shawls.

The time is 9:45. At midnight Nikola Tesla will produce his greatest miracle. The number twelve seems auspicious. It is important to him, for reasons he cannot understand, that it is divisible by three.

Anne Morgan, daughter of financier J. Pierpoint Morgan, stands at a little distance from his table. Though still in finishing school she is tall, self-possessed, strikingly attractive. She is reluctant to disturb Tesla, knowing he prefers to dine alone. Still she is drawn to him irresistibly. He is rake thin and handsome as the devil himself, with steel gray eyes that pierce through to her soul.

"Mr. Tesla," she says, "I pray I am not disturbing you."

Tesla looks up, smiles gently. "Miss Morgan." He begins to rise.

"Please, do not get up. I was merely afraid I would miss you. I
had hoped we might walk together after you finished here."

"I would be delighted."

"I shall await you there, by the Basin."

She withdraws. Trailing a gloved hand along the balustrade, she
tries to avoid the drunken crowds which swarm the Exposition
Grounds. Tomorrow the Fair will close and pass into history. Already
there are arguments as to what is to become of these splendid buildings. There is neither money to maintain them nor desire to demol-
ish them. Chicago's Mayor, Carter Harrison, worries that they will
end up filthy and vandalized, providing shelter for the hundreds of
poor who will no longer have jobs when the Fair ends.

Her thoughts turn back to Tesla. She finds herself inordinately
taken with him. At least part of the attraction is the mystery of his
personal life. At age 37 he has never married nor been engaged. She
has heard rumors that his tastes might be, to put it delicately, Greek
in nature. There is no evidence to support this gossip and she does
not credit it. Rather it seems likely that no one has yet been willing
to indulge the inventor's many idiosyncrasies.

She absently touches her bare left ear lobe. She no longer wears
the pearl earrings that so offended him on their first meeting. She
flushes at the memory, and at that point Tesla appears.

"Shall we walk?" he asks.

She nods and matches his stride, careful not to take his arm. Tesla
is not comfortable with personal contact.

To their left is the Hall of Agriculture. She has heard that its
most popular attraction is an 11-ton cheese from Ontario. Like so
many other visitors to the Fair, she has not actually visited any of the
exhibits. They seem dull and pedestrian compared to the purity and
classical lines of the buildings which house them. The fragrance of
fresh roses drifts out through the open doors, and for a moment she
is lost in a reverie of New York in the spring.

As they pass the end of the hall they are in darkness for a few
moments. Tesla seems to shudder. He has been silent and intent, as if
compulsively counting his steps. It would not surprise her if this
were actually the case.

"Is anything wrong?" she asks.

"No," Tesla says. "It's nothing."

In fact the darkness is full of lurking nightmares for Tesla. Just now he was five years old again, watching his older brother Daniel fall to his death. Years of guilty self-examination have not made the scene clearer. They stood together at the top of the cellar stairs, and then Daniel fell into the darkness. Did he fall? Did Nikola, in a moment of childish rage, push him?

All his life he has feared the dark. His father took his candles away, so little Nikola made his own. Now the full-grown Tesla has brought electric light to the White City, carried by safe, inexpensive alternating current. It is only the beginning.

They round the East end of the Court of Honor. At the Music Hall, the Imperial Band of Austria plays melodies from Wagner. Anne Morgan shivers in the evening chill. "Look at the moon," she says. "Isn't it romantic?"

Tesla's smile seems condescending. "I have never understood the romantic impulse. We humans are meat machines, and nothing more."

"That is hardly a pleasant image."

"I do not mean to be offensive, only accurate. That is the aim of science, after all."

"Yes, of course," Anne Morgan says. "Science." There seems no way to reach him, no chink in his cool exterior. This is where the others gave up, she thinks. I will prove stronger than all of them. In her short, privileged existence, she has always obtained what she wants. "I wish I knew more about it."

"Science is a pure, white light," Tesla says. "It shines evenly on all things, and reveals their particular truths. It banishes uncertainty, and opinion, and contradiction. Through it we master the world."

They have circled back to the west, and to their right is the Liberal Arts Building. She has heard that it contains so much painting and sculpture that one can only wander helplessly among it. To attempt to seek out a single artist, or to look for the French Impressionists, of whom she has been hearing so much, would be sheer futility.

Under Tesla's electric lights, the polished facade of the building sparkles. For a moment, looking down the impossibly long line of perfect Corinthian columns, she feels what Tesla feels: the triumph of man over nature, the will to conquer and shape and control. Then the night breeze brings her the scent of roses from across the Basin and the feeling passes.

THEY ENTER the Electricity Building together and stand in the center, underneath the great dome. This is the site of the Westinghouse exhibit, a huge curtained archway resting upon a metal platform. Beyond the arch are two huge Tesla coils, the largest ever built. At the peak of the arch is a tablet inscribed with the words: WESTINGHOUSE ELECTRIC & MANUFACTURING CO./TESLA POLYPHASE SYSTEM.

Tesla's mood is triumphant. Edison, his chief rival, has been proven wrong. Alternating current will be the choice of the future. The Westinghouse company has this week been awarded the contract to build the first two generators at Niagara Falls. Tesla cannot forgive Edison's hiring of Menlo Park street urchins to kidnap pets, which he then electrocuted with alternating current—"Westinghoused" them, as he called it. But Edison's petty, lunatic attempts to discredit the polyphase system have failed, and he stands revealed as an old, bitter, and unimaginative man.

Edison has lost, and history will soon forget him.

George Westinghouse himself, Tesla's patron, is here tonight. So are J.P. Morgan, Anne's father, and William K. Vanderbilt and Mayor Harrison. Here also are Tesla's friends Robert and Katharine Johnson, and Samuel Clemens, who insists everyone call him by his pen name.

It is nearly midnight.

Tesla steps lightly onto the platform. He snaps his fingers and gas-filled tubes burst into pure white light. Tesla has fashioned them to spell out the names of several of the celebrities present, as well as the names of his favorite Serbian poets. He holds up his hands to the awed and expectant crowd. "Gentlemen and Ladies. I have no wish to bore you with speeches. I have asked you here to witness a demonstration of the power of electricity."

He continues to talk, his voice rising to a high pitch in his excitement. He produces several wireless lamps and places them around the stage. He points out that their illumination is undiminished, despite their distance from the broadcast power source. "Note how the gas at low pressure exhibits extremely high conductivity. This gas is little different from that in the upper reaches of our atmosphere."

He concludes with a few fireballs and pinwheels of light. As the applause gradually subsides he holds up his hands once again. "These are little more than parlor tricks. Tonight I wish to say thank you, in a dramatic and visible way, to all of you who have supported me through your patronage, through your kindness, through your friendship. This is my gift to you, and to all of mankind."

He opens a panel in the front of the arch. A massive knife switch is revealed. Tesla makes a short bow and then throws the switch.

The air crackles with ozone. Electricity roars through Tesla's body. His hair stands on end and flames dance at the tips of his fingers. Electricity is his God, his best friend, his only lover. It is clean, pure, absolute. It arcs through him and invisibly into the sky. Tesla alone can see it. To him it is blinding white, the color he sees when inspiration, fear, or elation strikes him.

The coils draw colossal amounts of power. All across the great hall, all over the White City, lights flicker and dim. Anne Morgan cries out in shock and fear.

Through the vaulted windows overhead the sky itself begins to glow.

Something sparks and hisses and the machine winds down. The air reeks of melted copper and glass and rubber. It makes no difference. The miracle is complete.

Tesla steps down from the platform. His friends edge away from him, involuntarily. Tesla smiles like a wise father. "If you will follow me, I will show you what man has wrought."

Already there are screams from outside. Tesla walks quickly to the doors and throws them open.

Anne Morgan is one of the first to follow him out. She cannot help but fear him, despite her attraction, despite all her best intentions. All around her she sees fairgoers with their necks craned upward, or their eyes hidden in fear. She turns her own gaze to the heavens and lets out a short, startled cry.

The sky is on fire. Or rather, it burns the way the filaments burn in one of Tesla's electric lamps. It has become a sheet of glowing white. After a few seconds the glare hurts her eyes and she must look away.

It is midnight, and the Court of Honor is lit as if by the noonday sun. She is close enough to hear Tesla speak a single, whispered word: "Magnificent."

Westinghouse comes forward nervously. "This is quite spectacular," he says, "but hadn't you best, er, turn it off?"

Tesla shakes his head. Pride shines from his face. "You do not seem to understand. The atmosphere itself, some 35,000 feet up, has become an electrical conductor. I call it my 'terrestrial night light.' The charge is permanent. I have banished night from the world for all time."

"For all time?" Westinghouse stammers.

Anne Morgan slumps against a column, feels the cold marble against her back. Night, banished? The stars, gone forever? "You're mad," she says to Tesla. "What have you done?"

Tesla turns away. The reaction is not what he expected. Where is their gratitude? He has turned their entire world into a White City, a city in which crime and fear and nightmares are no longer possible. Yet men point at him, shouting curses, and women weep openly.

He pushes past them, toward the train station. Meat machines, he thinks. They are so used to their inefficient cycles of night and day. But they will learn.

He boards a train for New York and secures a private compartment. As he drives on into the white night, his window remains brilliantly lighted.

In the light there is truth. In the light there is peace. In the light he will be able, at last, to sleep.

LANGUAGE

TOM HEARD his office door click shut. He looked up and saw her and his palms started to sweat.

Her name was Jennifer. She was maybe eighteen. Her blonde perm had grown out dark at the roots and her eyes showed a little too much white around the irises. It gave her a wanton look that Tom had tried to ignore all semester.

"Is it true," she asked, "what you said in class this morning? About the Malaysians?" She sat down across from his desk and slouched until her neck hit the back of the chair.

"The Malay," Tom said. "Yes, it's true." It seemed there was only one word for food in Malay, and it could mean anything from "this is my lunch" to "eat me." It was the sort of one-liner meant to keep the attention of an eight-o'clock Freshman Comp section, not something Tom wanted brought up to him afterward.

"I just don't understand," Jennifer said. "I mean, how do they ever know what they're saying to each other?"

Tom couldn't keep his own signals straight. Jennifer's legs had drifted apart, and Tom could see her long thighs disappear up the shadowed legs of her bermuda shorts. Is this an accident? Tom thought. Is she really coming on to me? It felt like an accident. Like a car crash, happening in slow motion.

"Well," Tom said. "Maybe you'd want to do a little research on it. Think about it for your term paper."

"I'd probably need a lot of help."

She seemed to touch the end of her tongue to her upper lip. There were trees all around the building, blooming furiously, and the room was too shawdowy for Tom to be sure of anything. "One place you might start," Tom said, "is to look at the way language can also *expand* concepts." In the charged atmosphere his words had begun to take on double meanings. "Like the Eskimo. The Innuit have six different words for walrus, depending on age, strength, sex…uh, all those kinds of things. An *ipiksaulik* is a two-year old, male or… female. A *timartik* is a large male. And so on. For example, they don't have a word that just means 'snow.' There's a different word for every kind."

"That's really amazing," Jennifer said. "How do you know all this stuff?" She crossed her legs, but at the same time her eyes widened and green-filtered sunlight glistened across them.

"It's useless, most of it," Tom said.

"I think it's fascinating."

"You want a research topic?" he asked her, suddenly gripped by a wild impulse, sheer sexual longing out of control. He recognized it, saw it every day in his classes. It was what made desperate boys wear hideous clothes and smash furniture at frat parties and shout insults out the windows of Trans Ams.

"Think," he said, "how a more specific language could change an entire society. Suppose, for example, English didn't have the phrase 'I love you.' Lots of languages don't. Spanish, for instance. Suppose we had fifty different, very specific, phrases instead. 'I like being seen with you in front of my friends,' or 'I just want to have great sex with you and not call you for three weeks,' or 'I need somebody around when I'm seventy and wrinkled and ugly and maybe you'd hang around that long,' or 'you seem to want some empty reassurance so here it is.'"

Jennifer turned sideways in the chair and put her head on her left hand. Tom could now see the white band of her bra as it passed under her right arm, and just a hint of the lace on the cup. His heart pounded so loud he wondered if Jennifer could hear it too.

"Or how about," he said, "'I want to sleep with you so you'll give me an A in your class.'"

She didn't flinch. He'd thought, maybe even hoped, it would send her out of the office in either rage or embarrassment. Instead she just sat there, with a smile he knew he would have to look at for the rest of the semester. Language had failed him again.

"I think that'll be all for today, Jennifer."

"Okay, Dr. Marsh," she said, getting up slowly. "See you in class."

LINDA HAD GONE to bed. Both kids had been tucked in hours ago. Tom walked around downstairs in the vague glow that trickled out of the kitchen. On one wall were the pots and fishing nets he'd brought back from the Mexican village where he'd done his dissertation. He'd spent a summer there fifteen years ago, recording what he could of a Mayan dialect from its last living speaker.

When Cortez arrived there had been over a thousand different languages spoken in the New World. Now there less than four hundred, and the number dropped every year. What English didn't destroy it corrupted; the words "OK" and "car" and "jeans" had become part of virtually every vocabulary on the planet.

Tom picked up a Mayan fishing club, his fingers reading the information in the hard, smooth wood of the handle. That, he thought, had been an adventure. Fucking an eighteen-year-old student was not an adventure. It was lunacy.

Of course it was. Then why did he feel like somebody had smeared Vick's Vapo-Rub all over his crotch?

LINDA LAY on her stomach, not quite asleep. Tom undressed and got in bed next to her. "Rub my back?" she asked drowsily.

"Sure," Tom said. He reached across with his right hand and idly worked the muscles in her neck. The touch and smell of her skin still excited him. Or maybe it was just residual lust from Jennifer. Not that it mattered. He knew he could make love to her, but he also knew she wasn't in the mood. It would mean laboring over her while she lay quietly with her eyes closed, and he wasn't in the mood for that himself.

At dinner she'd imitated an old woman from her office, made Tom laugh as hard as the kids. Afterwards he found she'd forgotten to grease the lasagna pan again and it had taken him twenty minutes to scrub off the carbonized sauce.

"Mmmmm," she said. A minute or so later she turned her head to face him and said, "I love you."

Tom stopped rubbing. She was asleep. "Yes, I know," he said to the darkness. "But what do you mean?"

MYSTERY TRAIN

For Bruce Sterling

A S HE CLIMBED the stairs, Elvis popped the cap off the pill bottle and shook a couple more Dexedrines into his palm. They looked like pink candy hearts, lying there. He tossed them into the back of his throat and swallowed them dry.

"Hey, Elvis, man, are you sure you want to keep taking those things?" Charlie was half a flight behind, drunk and out of breath. "I mean, you been flying on that shit all weekend."

"I can handle it, man. Don't sweat it." Actually the last round of pills hadn't affected him at all, and now his muscles burned and his head felt like a bowling ball. He collapsed in an armchair in the third floor bedroom, as far as possible from the noise of the reporters and the kids and the girls who always stood outside the house. "In three weeks we're out of here, man. Out of Germany, out of the Army, out of these goddamn uniforms." He untied his shoes and kicked them off.

"Amen, brother."

"Charlie, turn on the goddamn TV, will you?"

"Come on, man, that thing's got a remote control, and I ain't it."

"Okay, okay." Elvis lunged for the remote control box and switched on the brand-new RCA color console. It was the best money could buy, the height of American technology, even if Germany didn't have any color transmissions to pick up with it.

Charlie had collapsed across the bed. "Hey, Elvis. When you get home, man, you ought to get yourself three different TVs. I mean, you're the king, right? That way, not only can you fuck more girls than anybody and make more money than anybody and take more pills than anybody, you can watch more TV than anybody, too. You can have a different goddamn TV for every channel. One for ABC…" He yawned. "One for NBC…" He was asleep.

"Charlie?" Elvis said. "Charlie, you lightweight." He looked around the edge of the chair and saw Charlie's feet hanging off the end of the bed, heel up and perfectly still.

To hell with it, Elvis thought, flipping through the channels. Let him sleep. They'd had a rough weekend, driving into Frankfurt in the BMW and picking up some girls, skating on the icy roads all across the north end of Germany, hitting the booze and pills. In the old days it had annoyed Elvis mightily that his body couldn't tolerate alcohol, but ever since one of his sergeants had given him his first Dexedrine he hadn't missed booze at all. Charlie still liked the bottle, but for Elvis there was nothing like that rush of power he got from the pills.

Well, there was one thing, of course, and that was being on stage. It was not quite two years now since he'd been inducted—since Monday, March 24, 1958, and he'd been counting the days. The Colonel had said no USO shows, no nothing until he was out. Nobody got Elvis for free.

The Colonel had come to take the place of his mother, who had died while Elvis was still in basic, and his father, who had betrayed Gladys's memory by seeing other women. There was no one else that Elvis could respect, that he could look to for advice. If the Colonel said no shows then that was it.

Something flashed on the TV screen. Elvis backed through the dead channels to find it again, ending up with a screen full of electronic snow. He got up and played with the fine tuning ring to see if he could sharpen it any.

Memories of his early years haunted him. Those had been the best times, hitting the small towns with just Scotty and Bill, the equipment strapped to the top of Scotty's brand-new, red-and-white '56 Chevy. Warming the audience up with something slow, like "Old Shep," then laying them out, ripping the joint with "Good Rockin' Tonight." Getting out of control, his legs shaking like he had epilepsy, forgetting to play the guitar, his long hair sticking out in front like the bill of a cap, taking that mike stand all the way to the floor and making love to it, shaking and sweating and feeling the force and power of the music hit those kids in the guts like cannon fire.

He gave up on the TV picture and paced the room, feeling the first pricklings of the drug. His eyelids had started to vibrate and he could feel each of the individual hairs on his arms.

When he sat down again there was something on the screen.

It looked like a parade, with crowds on both sides of the street and a line of cars approaching. They were black limousines, convertibles, with people waving from the back seats. Elvis thought he recognized one of the faces, a Senator from up north, the one everybody said was going to run for President.

He tried the sound. It was in German and he couldn't make any sense of it. The only German words he'd learned had been in bed, and they weren't the kind that would show up on television.

The amphetamine hit him just as the senator's head blew apart.

Elvis watched the chunks of brain and blood fly through the air in slow motion. For a second he couldn't believe what he was seeing, then he jumped up and grabbed Charlie by the shoulder.

"Charlie, wake up! C'mon man, this is serious!" Charlie rolled onto his back, eyes firmly shut, a soft snore buzzing in his throat. No amount of shaking could wake him up.

On the television, men in dark suits swarmed over the car as it picked up speed and disappeared down the road. The piece of film ran out, hanging in the projector for a moment, then the screen turned white.

He went back to the chair and stood with his hands resting on its high, curved back. Had he really seen what he thought he saw? Or was it just the drugs? He dug his fingers into the dingy gray-green fabric of the chair, the same fabric that he'd seen by the mile all through Europe. He was tired of old things: old chairs, old wood-floored houses, Frau Gross, the old woman who lived with them, the old buildings and cobbled streets of Bad Nauheim.

America, he thought, here I come. Clean your glass and polish your chrome and wax your linoleum tile.

The TV flickered and showed a hotel room with an unmade bed and clothes all around. On the nightstand was an overflowing ashtray and an empty bottle. Elvis recognized the Southern Comfort label even in the grainy picture. A woman sat on the floor with her back against the bed. She had ratty hair and flabby, pinched sort of face. The nipples of her small breasts showed through her T-shirt, which looked like somebody had spilled paint and bleach all over it.

Elvis thought she must be some kind of down-and-out hooker. He was a little disgusted by the sight of her. Still he couldn't look away as she brought a loaded hypodermic up to her arm and found a vein.

Static shot across the screen and the image broke up. Diagonal lines scrolled past a field of fuzzy gray. Elvis felt the Dexedrine bounce his heart against the conga drum of his chest. He sat down to steady himself, his fingers rattling lightly against the arm of the chair.

"Man," Elvis said to the room, "I am really fucked up."

A new voice came out of the TV. It must have originally belonged to some German girl, breathy and sexual, but bad recording had turned it into a mechanical whisper. Another room took shape, another rumpled bed, this one with a black man lying in it, long frizzy hair pressed against the pillow, a trickle of vomit running out of his mouth. He bucked twice, his long, muscular fingers clawing at the air, and lay still.

Elvis pushed the heels of his hands into his burning eyes. It's the drugs, he thought. The drugs and not sleeping and knowing I'm going home in a couple of weeks...

He wandered into the hall, one hand on the crumbling plaster wall to steady himself. He tried the handle on the room next to his but the door refused to open.

"Red? Hey, Red, get your ass up and answer this door." He slapped the wood a couple of times and then gave up, afraid to deal with Frau Gross when he was so far gone. He went into the bathroom instead and splashed cold water on his face, letting it soak the collar of his shirt. He wouldn't miss this screwy European plumbing, either.

"I feel so good," he sang to himself, "I'm living in the USA..." He looked like shit. With his green fatigues and sallow skin he looked like a fucking Christmas tree, with two red ornaments where his eyes were supposed to be.

He went back to the bedroom and sat down again. He needed sleep. He'd find something boring, like Bonanza in German, and maybe he could doze off in the chair.

As he reached for the remote, another film started. It was scratched and grainy and not quite in focus. Some fat guy in a white suit was hanging on to a mike stand and mumbling. It was impossible to understand what he said, especially with the nasal German narration that ran on top. Elvis made out a lot of "you knows" and "well, wells."

The camera moved in and Elvis went cold. Despite his age and his blubber and his long, girlish hair, the guy was trying to do an Elvis imitation. A band started up in the background and the fat man began to sing.

The Colonel had warned him this might happen. You don't drop out for two years and not expect somebody to try and cut you. Bobby Darin with all his finger-popping and that simpering Ricky Nelson had been bad enough, but this was really the end. Elvis had never heard the song that the fat guy was trying to sing. He was obviously being carried by the size of the orchestra behind him. Pathetic, Elvis thought. A joke. The fat guy curled his lip, threw a couple karate punches, and let one leg begin to shake.

Dear God, Elvis thought.

It wasn't possible.

Elvis lurched out of the chair and yanked Charlie out of bed by the ankles. "Wha...?" Charlie moaned.

"Get up. Get up and look at this shit."

Charlie struggled to a sitting position and scrubbed his eyes with his hands. "I don't see nothing."

"On the TV, man. You got eyes in your head?"

"There's nothing there, man. Nothing."

Elvis turned, saw snowy interference blocking out the signal again. "Get a chair," Elvis said.

"Aw, man, I'm really whacked..."

"Get the goddamn chair."

Elvis sat back in front of the TV, his heels pounding jump time against the hardwood floor. He heard Charlie dragging a chair up the stairs as the screen cleared and a caption flashed below the singer's face.

Rapid City, South Dakota, it said.

June, 1977.

Elvis didn't know he was on his feet, didn't know he had the service automatic in his hand until his finger went tight on the trigger.

Huge white letters filled the screen.

ELVIS, they said.

He fired. The roar of the gun seemed make the entire building jump. The picture tube blew in with a sharp crack and a shower of glass. Sparks hissed out on the floor and a single breath of sour smoke wafted out of the ruined set.

Elvis felt the room buzz with hostile forces. He had to get out. Charlie stood in the doorway, staring open-mouthed at the ruins of the set as Elvis shoved past him, letting the gun drop from his nerveless fingers and clatter across the floor. It wasn't until he was downstairs and the cold air hit him that he realized he'd left his shoes and coat inside. The sidewalk was slick with ice and a mixture of sleet and rain fell as he stood there, eyes jerking back and forth, fingers twitching, legs tensed to run and go on running.

It had to be a mistake, he thought. Something from a burlesque show over in Frankfurt, maybe. Somebody had just screwed up the titles, gotten the date wrong.

Yeah, and the name wrong too.

The silence closed in on him. For the first time since they'd moved into the house on Goethestrasse there weren't any people on the street. In the distance, whining high and faint like a mosquito's wings, he heard a motorcycle approaching. It was the only sound in the night.

He started to feel the cold. Still it wasn't bad enough to make him go back inside, to face the empty, staring socket of the TV set. He shivered, lifted one foot off the icy pavement.

A light winked at him from the end of the street. The motorcycle, coming toward him, rattled like machine gun fire and echoed off the wet streets and flat brick walls. It was moving too fast for the icy roads and the driver seemed barely in control. He slid in and out of the streetlamps' circles of light, shadowy in leather and denim.

Something like a premonition made Elvis start to turn and run back inside. The cold had numbed him and he couldn't seem to get the message through to his legs.

The bike skidded to a stop in front of the house and its engine died.

For a second Elvis and the rider started at each other in the silent moonlight. The rider had no helmet or goggles, just a pair of round, tortoise-shell glasses. Frost and bits of ice had clumped in his hair and the creases of his jacket. A cigarette hung out of the corner of his mouth, and Elvis was sure that if he could have seen the man's face he would have recognized him.

But the man's face was gone. Scars flowed and branched like rivers across the dead white skin of his cheeks. He had no eyebrows, and patches of hair were missing from his temples and forehead. One eye was permanently half-closed and the other was low enough to throw the ruined face off balance. The nose was little more than a flat place and the mouth smiled on one side and frowned on the other.

"Hey," the rider said.

"What?" Elvis was startled by the man's American accent.

"Hey, man. What happened to your shoes?"

The voice was maddeningly familiar. "Who are you?"

"You look shook, man." The scarred mouth stretched in what might have been a grin. "Like, 'All Shook Up,' right?"

"Dean," Elvis said, stunned. "Jimmy Dean, the actor."

The rider shrugged.

"You're dead," Elvis said. "I saw the pictures in the paper. That car was torn to pieces, man."

Dean, if that was truly who it was, touched the underside of his mutilated eye and rubbed it softly, as if remembering pain that Elvis could not even imagine.

"What are you doing here?"

Dean shrugged again. "They just, like, wanted me to come by and check up on you. It looks like you already got the message." He rose up on the bike, about to kick the starter, and Elvis moved toward him.

"Wait! Who's 'they?' What do you know about..." He stopped himself. Dean couldn't possibly know anything about what Elvis had seen on TV.

"Hey, be cool, man. If they wanted you to know who they were, then they would tell you, dig? I mean, they didn't even tell me shit, you know?" Dean looked him over. "But I can take a guess, man. I can take a real good guess what they want with you. I seen you on TV, the way you shake your legs and all that. The way you dress like a spade and sing all those raunchy songs. You scare people, man. People think you want to fuck all their daughters and turn their sons into hoods. They don't like that, man."

"I never tried to scare nobody," Elvis said.

Dean giggled. Coming out of that scarred mouth, it was terrifying. "Yeah, right. That's what I used to say."

"What do you mean? Are you threatening me?"

"No threats, man. You're the King. You know? You're the fucking King of America. King of all the cheeseburgers and pink Cadillacs and prescription drugs and handguns in the greatest country in the world. Shit, you are America. They don't have to threaten you. They don't have to hurt you. Just a little nudge here and a nudge there, and you'll fall right in line."

A door slammed and Charlie came staggering down the sidewalk. "Elvis? What the fuck, man?"

Dean looked like he wanted to say something else, then changed his mind. He started the bike, hunched his shoulders, and sped away.

"Jesus Christ," Charlie said. "You know who that was?"

"It was nobody," Elvis said. He put his hand in the middle of Charlie's chest and shoved him back toward the house. "Understand? It was nobody."

"There's going to be a new Elvis, brand new. I don't think he will go back to sideburns or ducktails. He's twenty-five now, and he has genuine adult appeal. I think he's going to surprise everyone…"

—COLONEL TOM PARKER, on Elvis's return from Germany

During rehearsals Elvis kept the windows of his hotel room covered with aluminum foil. It kept out the light and there was something comforting about having it there. It might even keep his TV set from picking up weird, lying broadcasts that would mess with his head. Just in case, he kept a loaded .45 on the bedside table, ready to blow the whole thing away. When forced to go out of the hotel, he kept his bodyguards with him at all times, the ones the papers had started to call his "Memphis Mafia."

He stayed inside as much as he could. The Florida air was hot and dead, seemed to pull the life right out of him. It had been the same in California and Las Vegas, everywhere he'd been since he came home from Germany. Everything was dry and hot and still. He was starting to believe it would be dry and hot and still forever.

As they taped the opening of the show he fought, without much success, to control his unease. They had him in his Army uniform again, walking out onstage to shake hands with Sinatra and his entire Rat Pack, all of them in tuxedos, mugging the camera, slapping each other on the back.

Over and over he caught himself thinking: What am I doing here?

He worked his way through the crowd, the faces blurring together into single entity with Bishop's mocking smile, Davis's processed hair and hideous rings, Lawford's limp handshake and Martin's whiskey breath. He had to learn to be comfortable with them. The Colonel had told him how it was going to be, and it was far too late to argue with the Colonel.

It happened while they were taping his duet with Sinatra, Sinatra who had called rock and roll "phony" and the singers "goons" just a couple of years before. Now they were trading verses, Elvis singing "Witchcraft" and Sinatra doing "Love Me Tender."

The scream came from somewhere toward the front of the audience. "That's not him!" It was a girl's voice, and it sounded at least as frightened as it was angry. The stage lights were blinding and Elvis couldn't see her face. "That's not Elvis!" she screamed. "What did you do with him?" The orchestra stopped and the girl's voice carried on unaccompanied. "Where is he? Where's Elvis?"

Elvis saw Sinatra make a gesture toward the wings. A moment later there were muffled noises from the audience and then a vast and empty silence.

"Don't worry," Sinatra said. "You're one of us now. We'll take good care of you."

"Yes, sir." Elvis nodded and closed his eyes. "Yes, sir," he said.

THE WAR AT HOME

TEN OF US in the back of a Huey, assholes clenched like fists, C-rations turned to sno-cones in our bellies. Tracers float up at us, swollen, sizzling with orange light, like one dud firecracker after another. Ahead of us the gunships pound Landing Zone Dog with everything they have, flex guns, rockets, and 50-calibers, while the artillery screams overhead and the Air Force A1-Es strafe the clearing into kindling.

We hover over the LZ in the sudden phosphorus dawn of a flare, screaming, "Land, motherfucker, land!" while the tracers close in, the shell of the copter ticking like a clock as the thumb-sized rounds go through her, ripping the steel like paper, splattering somebody's brains across the aft bulkhead.

Then falling into knee-high grass, the air humming with bullets and stinking of swamp ooze and gasoline and human shit and blood. Spinning wildly, my finger jamming down the trigger of the M-16, not caring anymore where the bullets go.

And waking up in my own bed, Clare beside me, shaking me, hissing, "Wake up, wake up for Christ's sake."

I sat up, the taste of it still in my lungs, hands twitching with berserker frenzy. "'M okay," I said. "Nightmare. I was back in Nam."

"What?"

"Flashback," I said. "The war."

"What are you talking about? You weren't in the war."

I looked at my hands and remembered. It was true. I'd never been in the Army, never set foot in Vietnam.

THREE MONTHS EARLIER we'd shot an Eyewitness News series on Vietnamese refugees. His name was Nguyen Ky Duk, former ARVN colonel, now a fry cook at Jack in the Box. "You killed my country," he said. "All of you. Americans, French, Japanese. Like you would kill a dog because you thought it might have, you know, rabies. Just kill it and throw it in a ditch. It was a living thing and now it is dead."

THE AFTERNOON of the massacre we got raw footage over the wire. About a dozen of us crowded the monitor and stared at the shattered windows of the Safeway, the mounds of cartridges, the bloodstains, the puddles of congealing food.

"What was it he said?"

"Something about 'gooks.' 'You're all fucking gooks, just like the others, and now I'll kill you too,' something like that."

"But he wasn't in Nam. They talked to his wife."

"So why'd he do it?"

"He was a gun nut. Black market stuff, like that M-16 he had. Camo clothes, the whole nine yards. A nut."

I walked down the hall, past the potted ferns and bamboo, and bought a Coke from the machine. I could still remember the dream, the feel of the M-16 in my hand. The rage. The fear.

"LIKE IT?" Clare asked. She turned slowly, the loose folds of her black cotton pajamas fluttering, her face hidden by the conical straw hat.

"No," I said. "I don't know. It makes me feel weird."

"It's fashion. Fashion's supposed to make you feel weird."

I let myself through the sliding glass door, into the back yard. The grass had grown a foot or more without my noticing, and strange plants had come up between the flowers, suffocating them in sharp fronds and broad green leaves.

"DID YOU GO?"

"No," I said. "I was I-Y. Underweight, if you can believe it." In fact I was losing weight again, my muscles turning stringy under sallow skin.

"Me either. My dad got a shrink to write me a letter. I did the marches, Washington and all that. But you know something? I feel funny about not going. Kind of guilty, somehow. Even though we shouldn't ever have been there, ever though we were burning villages and fragging our own guys. I feel like…I don't know. Like I missed something. Something important."

"Maybe not," I said. Through cracked glass I could see the sunset thicken the trees.

"What do you mean?"

I shrugged. I wasn't sure myself. "Maybe it's not too late," I said.

I WALK THROUGH the haunted streets of my town, sweltering in the January heat. The jungle arches over me; children's voices in the distance chatter in their odd pidgin Vietnamese. The TV station is a crumbling ruin and none of us feel comfortable there any longer. We work now in a thatched hut with a mimeo machine.

The air is humid, fragrant with anticipation. Soon the planes will come and it will begin in earnest.

KIDDING AROUND

MOM PULLED OUT the fake vomit again yesterday. It's been almost a year and I thought maybe she was over all that. Guess not, huh?

We were in the doctor's office. I'd just had a checkup so I could stay on the Pill. I'm not on it because of *that,* it's because my periods are messed up. Like there's somebody whose periods are normal? Could I see a show of hands, please? Mom is paying the bill. She waits until the nurse looks away for something and plop, drops it right there on the linoleum. Then she goes into her act.

"Oh, Miss?" holding a handkerchief to her nose. "Miss? Don't you think you should do something about this? I mean, this is a doctor's office, and how healthy can it be," and on and on. I have to admit it's a little hard not to crack up when I see the nurse's face. The nurse has her hands up and fluttering around and runs out front, turning green like she's going to lose it herself. Mom gets That Look and says, "Well, if you won't do anything about it, I guess I'll have to take care of it myself," and sweeps it up with her handkerchief. She says, "Come along dear," and we're out the door.

This is pretty typical. It can go on for weeks. One time last year she drove me and my little brother Ricky to Houston for a speech tournament. Everybody was there, my best friend Gail, even this guy Ryan who I'm not really interested in, but is as close to cute as they get in Tomball, Texas. So my Mom dresses up in a clown costume. I'm *not* kidding. Purple wig, red ball nose, big net collar, the works. And in case there isn't anybody in the entire city who hasn't already noticed that I came with her, she pulls out this three-foot bicycle horn and honks goodbye to me with it.

My Dad's not any better. He doesn't carry around itching powder and Chinese finger traps, but he's never serious either. What kills me is he won't ever admit to anything. He'll like leave a *Playboy* centerfold around and there'll be something really gross written to him on it, like it was from the girl in the picture. Mom yells at him and he just shrugs and says, "Well, *somebody* did it."

Gail has been my best friend since I was three years old. She lives on the other side of the highway from me. We're totally different people. I'm kind of big-boned but I have a pretty okay face, just wear a little eye shadow and lipstick. Gail is short and blond and dresses to the max every day. All she really wants out of life is to marry some cute guy in Houston with a lot of money and a fast car. But that's okay. She'll be my best friend until I die. How can I make new friends when I don't dare bring them home? Gail is at least used to whoopie cushions and plastic ice cubes with flies or cockroaches inside.

When I sat down to eat with Gail today I found a note in my lunch that said, "I fixed your favorite, peanut butter and maggots. Love, Mom." I peel my banana and it falls apart in sections. Gail's seen it a hundred times but it still makes her laugh.

"Your Mom is so weird," she says.

"No kidding."

"At least you've got your hearing left." Gail's Mom plays this sixties music at unbelievable volume all day and night. Gail's absolutely most shameful secret is that she was originally named Magic Mountain. I'm *not* kidding. Her first day at school she told everybody she was named Gail. Only she didn't know how to spell it, and wrote it G-A-L. I had to take her aside and explain. Anyway, she kept on her Mom about it until her Mom finally made it legal. Nobody else remembers all that, but I do.

Everybody's parents seem to think the sixties were this unbelievably wonderful time. They even have TV shows and everything about it now. What I can't understand is, if it was so wonderful, why did they stop? Why don't they still wear long hair and bell-bottoms and madras or whatever it was? I don't think it was the sixties. I think they just liked being young.

Which is more than I can say. "Mom's into the plastic vomit again," I tell Gail.

"Oh God. Geez, you know, I can't come over this afternoon after all. I just remembered this really important stuff I have to do."

"Thanks, Gail. Thanks a lot. That means I'll be stuck at home alone with her."

"What about Ricky?"

"He'll spend the night at the Jameson's. At the first sight of novelty items he's out the door, and Dad with him."

"I saw him this morning, did I tell you?"

"Ricky?"

"Your dad."

"No. Where was this?"

She looked sorry she brought it up. "Oh, it wasn't anything. I just saw him when Mom drove me to school."

I wanted to say, if it wasn't anything, then why did you bring it up, dork-brain? But she looked embarrassed and a little scared so I let it drop.

When I got home Mom was already in the kitchen. You can imagine my nervousness. Among the delights she's cooked when she's in a mood like this are: lemon meringue enchiladas, steak a la mode, chili con cookies, and banana pizza. The pizza was actually not too bad, but you understand what I'm saying.

We all sit down at the table. Mom brings out this big aluminum tray with a cover over it, like in the movies. She takes the cover off with a big flourish and goes, "Ta da!"

It's a casserole dish with what looks like overcooked brownies inside. We all stare at it.

"Eat," Mom says. "Come on, eat!"

No one wants to go first. Finally Ricky breaks down and pokes at it with a fork. It makes this nasty grinding sound. "Oh gross," he says. He looks more tired than really disgusted. Not like the time Mom walked around with the plastic dog mess on a Pamper, eating a piece of fudge. I lean over for a look myself.

"Mom," I say, "this is a mud pie." I sniff at it. It really *is* mud. Dried, baked mud now. "This is like not funny."

"If you don't eat every bite, you don't get dessert."

"You're slipping, Mom," Ricky says. "You're losing it. This is not even remotely funny. I'm going to the Jamesons'. If I hurry, maybe I'll be in time for supper."

Dad is just staring off into the corner, holding onto his chin. It's like he's not really there at all.

I went into the den and put on MTV. If there was a God it would have been Al TV, but it wasn't. I think Weird Al Yankovic is the greatest thing in the world. He plays the accordion and does goofed-up versions of songs, in case you've never heard of him. I saw him in concert in Houston and broke through his bodyguards so I could hug him.

I watched TV for a while and then Mom came in dressed in a maid's costume and started dusting. She has this huge feather duster, a joke feather duster, so big she can hardly move it around without knocking things over. Dad comes in and says to me, "Let's go for a burger."

I was glad to get away. That mud pie business was just *too* weird. We got in his pickup and headed for the Wendy's just down the highway. Outside the pickup is Tomball, Texas in all its glory. Flat, except for the gullies, brown except for the trash. In a little over a year I go to college and I won't ever look back.

"Gail said she saw you this morning," I tell him.

"She could have, I suppose."

"She was real weird about it. She acted like she shouldn't have told me. Do you know why that is?"

He rolls his window down with one hand, and makes a big deal out of scratching his head, real casual, you know, with the other. He's pretending not to pay any attention to the road, only he's really steering with his knee.

"Were you doing something you weren't supposed to do, Dad? Were you *with* somebody? Is that why Mom's acting weird? Because it's really hard to be in this family, you know? I mean, at any minute it could hit me. I could get this irresistible craving for an exploding cigar. It could be like diabetes. One minute I'm fine, the next I'm filling up my pockets with plastic ants. So I want you to tell me. Did you do something?"

He cranes his head out the window and drives for a while that way, then settles back into his seat. He shrugs. "*Somebody* did."

STEAM ENGINE TIME

THE KID turned up the gaslight in his room. The pink linen wall-paper still looked a little dingy. Ever since J. L. Driskill had opened his new place in December of '86 the Avenue Hotel had been going downhill.

There was a framed picture on the wall and the Kid had been staring at it for an hour. It was an engraving of a Pawnee Indian. The Indian's head was shaved except for a strip of hair down the middle. There were feathers in what hair he had, and it hung down over his forehead.

He compared it to what he saw in the mirror. He was pretty badly hung over from jimson weed and unlabeled whiskey the night before. His fine yellow hair went every which way and his eyes were mostly red. He got out his straight razor, stropped it a couple of times on his boot, and grabbed a hank of hair.

What the hell, he thought.

It was harder to do than he thought it would be, and he ended up with a lot of tiny cuts all over his head. When he was done he took the razor and used it to cut the bottom off his black leather duster coat. He hacked it off just below the waist. For a couple of seconds he wondered why in hell he was doing it, wondered if he'd lost his mind. Then he put it on and looked in the mirror again and this time he liked what he saw.

It was just right.

THERE'D BEEN A SALOON at the corner of Congress Avenue and Pecan Street pretty much from the time Austin changed its name from Waterloo and became the capital of Texas. These days it was called the Crystal Bar. There was an overhang right the way round the building, with an advertisement for Tom Moore's 10 cent cigars painted on the bricks on the Pecan Street side. The fabric of the carriages at the curb puffed out in the mild autumn breeze.

The mule cars were gone and the street cars were electric now, thanks to the dam that opened in May of the year before. They were calling Austin "the coming great manufacturing center of the Southwest." It was the Kid's first big city. The electric and telegraph wires strung all over downtown looked like the history of the future, block-printed across the sky.

The Kid was a half-hour late for a two-o'clock appointment with the Crystal's manager. The manager's name was Matthews, and he wore a bow tie and a starched collar and a tailormade suit. "Do you know 'Grand-Father's Clock is Too Tall for the Shelf?'" Matthews asked the Kid.

The Kid had kept his hat on. "Why sure I do." He took his steel-string Martin guitar out of the case and played it quiet with his fingers. "'It was bought on the morn of the day he was born/And was always his treasure and pride/But it stopped—short—never to go again/When the old man died.'"

I'm going to God-damned puke, the Kid thought.

"Not much of a voice," Matthews said.

"All I want is to pass the hat," the Kid said. "Sir."

"Not much of a hat, either. All right, son, you can try it. But if the crowd don't like it, you're out. Understand?"

"Yes sir," the Kid said. "I understand."

THE KID CAME BACK at nine that night. He'd bought some hemp leaves from a Mexican boy and smoked them but they didn't seem to help his nerves. It felt like Gentleman Jim Corbett was trying to punch his way out of the Kid's chest.

The ceiling must have been thirty feet high. The top half of the room was white with cigar smoke and the bottom half smelled like farts and spilled beer. Over half the tables and all but a couple of seats at the bar were full. The customers were all men, of course.

All white men. They said ladies dared not walk on the east side of the Avenue.

Nobody paid him much attention, least of all the waitresses. The Kid counted three of them. One of them was not all that old or used-up looking.

Some fat bastard in sleeve garters pounded out "The Little Old Cabin in the Lane" on a piano with a busted soundboard. The Kid knew the words. They talked about the days when "de darkies used to gather round de door/When dey used to dance an sing at night." If there was anything going to keep him from turning yellow and going back to the hotel, that had to be it.

There was a wooden stage about three feet wide and four feet high that ran across the back of the room. Just big enough for some fat tart to strut out on and hike up the back of her skirts. The Kid set the last vacant bar stool up on the stage with his guitar case. He climbed up and sat on the stool. It put him just high enough up to strangle on the cloud of smoke.

The piano player finished or gave up. Anyway he quit playing and went over to the bar. The Kid took out his guitar. He had a cord with a hook on the end that came up under the back and let him carry the weight of it on his neck. It was what they called a parlor guitar, the biggest one C. F. Martin and Sons made. With his copper plectrum and those steel strings it was loud as Jesus coming back. Still the Kid would have liked a bigger sound box. It would have made it even louder.

Somebody at the bar said, "Do you know 'Grand-Father's Clock'?"

"How about 'Ta-ra-ra-boom-de-ay?'" said somebody further down. The man was drunk and started singing it himself.

"No, 'Grand-Father's Clock!'" said another one. "Grand-Father's Clock!'"

The Kid took his hat off.

Maybe the whole bar didn't go quiet, but there was a circle of it for thirty or forty feet. The Kid looked at their faces and saw that he had made a mistake. It was the kind of mistake he might not live through.

There were upwards of fifty men looking at him. They all wore narrow brim hats and dark suits and the kind of thick mustaches

that seemed to be meant to hide their mouths in case they ever
accidentally smiled.

They were none of them smiling now.

The Kid didn't see any guns. But then none of them looked like
they needed a gun.

The Kid played a run down the bass strings and hit an E 7th as
hard as he could with his copper pick. "'Rolled and I tumbled,'" he
sang, "'cried the whole night long.'" He was so scared his throat was
swollen shut and his voice came out a croak. But his hand moved,
slapping the rhythm out of the guitar. The craziness came up in him
at the sound of it, to be playing that music here, in front of these
people, rubbing their faces in it, like it or not.

"'Rolled and I tumbled, lord,'" he sang, "'cried the whole
night long.'" He jumped off the stool and stomped the downbeat
with his bootheel. "'Woke up this morning, did not know right
from wrong.'"

He pounded through the chords again twice. He couldn't hold
still. He'd seen music do that to folks, lived with it all his life, share-
cropping in a black county with the families just one generation out
of slavery, seeing them around their bonfires on Saturday nights and
in their churches Sunday mornings, but this was the first time it had
ever happened to him.

It was time for a verse and he was so far gone all he could sing
was "Na na na na" to the melody line. When it came around again
he sang, "'Well the engine whistlin', callin' Judgment Day/I hear that
train a whistlin', callin' Judgment Day/When that train be pass by,
take all I have away.'"

Through the chords again. It was play or die or maybe both. The
song roared off the tracks and blew up on B 9th. The last notes hung
in the air for a long time. It was so quiet the Kid could hear the
wooden sidewalk creak as somebody walked by outside.

"Thank you," the Kid said.

One at a time they turned away and started talking to each other
again. A man in a plaid suit with watery blue eyes stared at him for
another few seconds and then hawked and spat on the floor.

"Thank you," the Kid said. "I'd now like to do one I wrote
myself. It's called 'Twentieth Century Man.' It's about how we got to

change with the times and not just let time get past us. It goes a little like this here." He started to hit the first chord but his right hand wouldn't move. He looked down. Matthews had a hold of it.

"Out," Matthews said.

"I was just getting 'em warmed up," the Kid said.

"Get the hell out," Matthews said, "or by thunder if they don't kill you I'll do it myself."

"I guess this means I don't pass the hat," the Kid said.

HE SAT ON the board sidewalk and wiped the sweat off the guitar strings. When he looked up the not-so-old waitress was leaning on the batwings, watching him.

"Was it supposed to be some kind of minstrel song?" she asked. "Like the Ethiopian Serenaders?"

"No," the Kid said. "It wasn't no minstrel song."

"Ain't heard nothin' like it before."

"Not supposed to have. Things everybody heard before is for shit. 'The Little Old Cabin in the Lane.' Songs like that make people the way they are."

"What way is that?"

"Ignorant."

"What happened to your hair?"

"Cut it."

"Why?"

"So it'd be different."

"Same with your coat?"

"That's right."

"You sure like things different."

"I guess I do."

"Where'd your song come from?"

"Back home."

"Where's that?"

"Mississippi."

"Well," she said. "I sort of liked it."

The Kid put the guitar back in the case. He shut the lid and closed the latches. "Thanks," he said. "You want to fuck?"

She looked at him like he was a dog just tried to pee on her shoe. She made the batwings bang together as she spun away hard and clomped away across the saloon.

THEY'D LAID AUSTIN out in a square. Streets named after Texas rivers went north and south, trees went east and west. The south side of the square lay along the Colorado River so they called it Water Avenue. There was West Avenue and North Avenue and East Avenue.

East of East Avenue was colored town. The Kid carried his guitar east down Bois d'Arc Street, pronounced BO-dark in Texas. Past East Avenue there weren't street lights any more. Babies sat barefoot in the street and there was music but it didn't seem to be coming from anywhere in particular. The air smelled like burned fat.

The Kid finally saw a bar and went inside. This time it got quiet for him right away. "Son," the man behind the bar said, "I think you in the wrong part of town."

"I want to play some music," the Kid said.

"Ain't no music here."

"They call it 'blue music.' You ever hear of it?"

The man smiled. "Didn't know music came in no colors. Now you run along, before you make a mistake and hurt you self."

HE WENT BACK to his hotel long enough to pack his bag and then he went down to the train station. He sat on a bench there and read a paper somebody had left behind. It was called *The Rolling Stone*. It seemed to be a lot of smart aleck articles about books and artists. There was a story by somebody called himself O. Henry. The Kid didn't find anything in there about music.

But then, what would you write about a song like "Grand-Father's Clock" or "The Little Old Cabin in the Lane?"

An old colored man pushed a broom back and forth, looking over at the Kid every once in a while. "Waitin' for a train?" the old man finally asked.

"That's right."

"Ain't no train for two hour."

"I know that."

He pushed his broom some more. "That your git-tar?" he asked after while.

"It is," the Kid said.

"Mind if I have me a look?"

The Kid took it out of the case and handed it to him. The old man sat next to the Kid on the bench. "Pretty thing, ain't it?"

"You play?" the Kid asked him.

"Naw," the old man said. He held the guitar like it was made out of soap and might squirt out of his hands if he squeezed down. "Well. Maybe I used to. Just a little. Ain't touched one in years, now."

"Go ahead," the Kid said. The old man shook his head and tried to hand the guitar back. The Kid wouldn't go for it. "I think maybe you could still play some."

"Think so?" the old man said. "Well, maybe."

He put his right thumb on the low E string and just let it sit there. After a while he fitted his left hand around the neck and pushed at the strings a little. "Oooo wee," he said. "*Steel* strings."

"That's right," the Kid said.

The old man closed his eyes. His head started to go back and for a second the Kid thought maybe the old man was drunk and fixing to pass out. Then the old man took a jack knife out of his pocket and set it on the knee of his jeans.

It made the Kid uncomfortable. He didn't think the old man was actually going to knife him over the guitar. But he couldn't see any other reason for the thing to be out.

The old man didn't open the blade. Instead he fitted the handle between the ring finger and little finger of his left hand. Then he ran it up and down the strings. It made an eerie sound, like a dying animal or a train whistle gone crazy.

Then the old man started to play.

The Kid had never heard anything like it. The notes howled and screamed and cried out bloody murder. The old man played till his fingers bled and the high E string broke in two.

When it was over the old man sat for a second, breathing heavy. Then he handed the guitar back. "Sorry about that string, son."

"Got me another one." Tears ran down the Kid's face. He didn't want to wipe them off. He thought maybe if he just left them alone the old man might not notice. "Where…where did you learn to do that?"

"Just somethin' I figured out for my own self. Don't mean nothin'."

"Don't mean nothin'? Why, that was the most beautiful thing I ever heard in my life."

"You know anything about steam engines?"

The Kid stared at him. A couple of seconds went by. "What?"

"Steam engines. Like on that locomotive you gonna be ridin'."

The Kid just shook his head.

"Well, they had all the pieces of that steam engine lyin' around for hundreds of years. Wasn't nobody knew what to do with 'em. Then one day five, six people up and invent a steam engine, all at the same time. Ain't no explanation for it. It was just steam engine time."

"I don't get it," the Kid said. "What are you tryin' to say?"

The old man stood up and pointed at the guitar. "Just that you lookin' for a life of misery, boy. Because the time for that thing ain't here yet."

JUST BEFORE DAWN, as the train headed west toward New Mexico, it started to rain. The Kid woke up to lightning stitched across the sky. It made him think about electric streetcars and electric lights. If electricity could make a light brighter, why couldn't it make a guitar louder? Then they'd have to listen.

He drifted back to sleep and dreamed of electric guitars.

SCALES

THERE'S A STANDARD rat behavior they call the Coolidge Effect. Back when I was a psych major, before I met Richard, before we got married, long before I had Emily, I worked in the lab 15 hours a week. I cleaned rat cages and typed data into the computer. The Coolidge Effect was one of those experiments that everybody had heard of but nobody had actually performed.

It seems if you put a new female in a male's cage, they mate a few times and go on with their business. If you keep replacing the female, though, it's a different story. The male will literally screw himself to death.

Someone supposedly told all this to Mrs. Calvin Coolidge. She said, "Sounds just like my husband."

IT STARTED IN JUNE, a few days after Emily's first birthday. I remember it was a Sunday night; Richard had to teach in the morning. I woke up to Richard moaning. It was a kind of humming sound, up and down the scale. It was a noise he made during sex.

I sat up in bed. As usual all the blankets were piled on my side. Richard was naked under a single sheet, despite the air conditioning. We'd fought about something that afternoon. I was still angry enough that I could find satisfaction in watching his nightmare.

He moved his hips up and down. I could see the little tent his penis made in the sheet. Clearly he was not squirming from fear. Just as I realized what was happening he arched his back and the sheet turned translucent. I'd never watched it before, not clinically like

that. It wasn't especially interesting and certainly not erotic. All I
could think of was the mess. I could smell it now, like water left
standing in an orange juice jar.

I lay down, facing away from him. The bed jolted as he woke up.
"Jesus," he whispered. I pretended to be asleep while he mopped up
the bed with some kleenex. In a minute or two he was asleep again.

I got up to check on Emily. She was face down in her crib, arms
and legs stretched out like a tiny pink bearskin rug. I touched her
hair, bent over to smell her neck. One tiny, perfect hand clutched at
the blanket under her.

"You missed it, Tater," I whispered. "You could have seen what
you've got to look forward to."

I MIGHT HAVE forgotten about it if Sally Keeler hadn't called that
Friday. Her husband had the office next to Richard's in the English
department.

"Listen," Sally said. "It's probably nothing at all."

"Pardon?"

"I thought somebody should let you know."

"Know what?"

"Has Richard been, I don't know, acting a little weird lately?"

For some reason I remembered his wet dream. "What do you
mean weird?"

Sally sighed dramatically. "It's just something Tony said last night.
Now Ann, I know you and Richard are having a few problems—
that's okay, you don't have to say anything—and I thought, well, a
real friend would come to you with this."

Sally was not a friend. Sally was someone who had been over to
dinner two or three times. I hadn't realized my marital problems
were such common knowledge. "Sally, will you get to the point?"

"Richard's been talking to Tony about this new grad student.
She's supposed to be from Israel or something."

"So?"

"So Richard was apparently just drooling over this girl. That
doesn't sound like him. I mean Richard doesn't even *flirt*."

"Is that all?"

"Well, no. Tony asked him what was the big deal and *Richard* said, 'Tony, you wouldn't believe it. You wouldn't believe it if I told you.' Those are like his exact words."

"Does this mystery woman have a name?"

"Lili, I think he said it was."

I tried to picture Richard, with his thinning hair and stubby little mustache, with his glasses and pot belly, sweeping some foreign sexpot off her feet.

Sally said, "It may not be anything at all."

One new associate professorship would open up next year. Richard and Tony were both in the running. Richard was generally thought to have the edge. "I'm sure you're right," I said. "I'm sure it's nothing at all."

"Hey, I wouldn't want to cause any problems."

"No," I said, "I'm sure you wouldn't."

THE NEXT WEDNESDAY Richard called to say he'd be home late. There was a visiting poet on campus for a reading. I looked it up in the paper. The reading was scheduled for eight.

At eight-thirty I put Emily in the station wagon and we drove over to the Fine Arts Center. We didn't find his car.

"Well, Tater," I said. "What do you think? Do we go across Central and check the hot sheet motels?"

She stared at me with huge, colorless eyes.

"You're right," I said. "We have too much pride for that. We'll just go home."

THERE WAS A COOKOUT that weekend at Dr. Taylor's. He was department chairman largely on the strength of having edited a Major American Writer in his youth. Now he had a drinking problem. His wife had learned that having parties at home meant keeping him off the roads.

The morning of the party I told Richard I wanted to go. By now he was used to my staying home from these things. I watched for signs of disappointment. He only shrugged.

"You'd better start trying to find a sitter," he said.

After dinner we began the slow, seemingly random movements that would inevitably end with the women in one part of the house and the men in another. Aleady most of the wives were downstairs, clearing up the soggy paper plates and empty beer bottles. I was upstairs with Jane Lang, the medievalist, and most of the husbands. Taylor had made a pejorative remark about women writers and everyone had jumped on him for it. Then Tony said, "Okay, I want to see everybody come up with a sexist remark they believe is true."

Taylor said, a little drunkenly, "Men have bigger penises than women."

Jane said, "Usually." Everyone laughed.

Robbie Shappard, who was believed to sleep with his students, said, "I read something the other day. There's this lizard in South America that's extinct now. What happened was another species of lizard came along that could perform the mating rituals better than the real females. The males all fucked the impostors. The chromosomes didn't match, of course, so no baby lizards. The whole species went toes up."

"Is that true?"

"I read it in the *Weekly World News,*" Robbie said. "It has to be true. What I want to know is, what does it mean?"

"That's easy," Jane said. "When it comes to sex, men don't know what's good for them."

"I think men and women are different species," Tony said.

"Too easy," Robbie said. "They've just got conflicting programs. When we were living in caves we had these drives designed to produce the maximum number of kids from the widest range of partners. The problem is we've still got those drives and they're not useful any more. That's what did those poor lizards in."

Tony said, "Okay, Ann. Your turn. Be serious, now."

"I don't know," I said. "I guess I subscribe to the old business about how women are more emotional."

"Emotional how?" Tony said. "Be specific."

"Right," Robbie said. "Be brief and specific. It's fifty percent of your grade riding on this."

I looked at Richard. He seemed distracted rather than contentious. "Well, men always seem concerned with exactitude, being able to measure things." There was some laughter, and I blushed. "You know. Like they don't want to say 'I'll love you forever.' They want to say, 'at current rates our relationship could reasonably be expected to continue at least another six months.' Whereas I would appreciate the gesture. Of saying 'forever.'"

Tony nodded. "Good one. Rich?"

"You want one? Okay. Here's what Robbie was trying to say earlier, only without the bullshit. Men want women and women want babies."

Everyone went quiet; it wasn't just me overreacting. The first thing I thought of was Emily. What did Richard mean? Did he not want her any more? Had he never wanted her? I'd heard that people felt this way when they were shot. No pain, only a sense of shock and loss, the knowledge that pain would surely follow.

"Speaking of babies," I said into the silence, "I should call home. Excuse me." I walked out of the room, looking for a phone, wanting most of all to be away from Richard.

I found a bathroom instead. I washed my face, put on fresh lipstick, and wandered downstairs. Sally found me there and raised an eyebrow. "Well?"

"Well what?"

"I assume you're here for a look at her."

"Who?"

"Lili. The mystery woman. All the men in the department are in love with her. Haven't you heard?"

"Is she here?"

Sally glanced around the room. I knew most of the women in the den with us. "I don't see her now. She was here a minute ago."

"What does she look like?"

"Oh, short, dark…sexy, I suppose. If you like eyeliner and armpit hair."

"What's she wearing?"

"Is that more than idle curiosity I hear in your voice? A tank top, a red tank top. And blue jeans. Very tight."

"Excuse me," I said, finally seeing the phone. "I have to call home."

The sitter answered on the second ring. Emily was asleep. There were no problems. "Okay," I said. I wanted to be home with her, to blow raspberries on her belly and feel her fingers in my hair. The silence had gone on too long. I said thank you and hung up.

I couldn't face going back upstairs. It would be a boy's club up there by now anyway. Fart jokes and cigars. A sliding glass door opened up to the back yard. I walked into the darkness, smelling summer in the cut grass and the lingering smoke from the grill.

Richard found me there when the party broke up. I was sitting in a lawn chair, watching the Dallas sky, which glows red all summer long. Something about all the lights and the polluted air.

"Nice move," Richard said. "Just walk right out on me, let the entire fucking party know our marriage is on the rocks."

"Is it?"

"What?"

"On the rocks. Our marriage. Are we splitting up?"

"Hell, I don't know. This isn't the time to ask, that's for sure. Oh no. Don't start. How are we supposed to walk out with you crying like that?"

"We'll go around the side of the house. Taylor's too drunk to know if we said goodnight or not. Answer my question."

"I said I don't know."

"Maybe we ought to find out."

"What does *that* mean?"

"Let's do whatever it is people do. See a counselor or something."

"Okay."

"Okay? That's all? Just 'okay'?"

"You're the one pushing for this, not me."

"Fine," I said, suddenly giddy. It was like standing on the edge of a cliff. Would I actually do something irreversible? Only Emily held me back. Then I looked at Richard again and thought, do I really want this man as her father?

"Fine," I said again. "Let's get out of here."

MY BEST FRIEND Darla had been divorced twice. She recommended a Mrs. McNabb.

"Oh God," I said. "It's going to be so expensive. Is it really going to help?"

"What do you care about help?" Darla said. "This is step one in getting rid of the creep. The rest gets easier. Believe me, it gets easier.

My second divorce was no worse than, oh, say, being in a body cast for six months."

I sat in front of the phone for a long time Monday. I was weighing the good and bad in our marriage and I was throwing anything I could find onto the scales. Everything on the good side had to do with money —the house, Richard's insurance, financial security. It wasn't enough.

I got us an appointment for the next morning. When I told Richard about it Monday night he looked surprised, as if he'd forgotten the whole wretched scene. Then he shrugged and said, "Okay, whatever."

We left Emily at the sitter's house. It was hard to let go of her. Richard kept looking at his watch. Finally we got away and drove downtown, to a remodeled prairie-style house off of East Grand.

Mrs. McNabb was five-eleven, heavy in the chest and hips, fifty years old with short hair in various shades of gray. No makeup, natural fiber clothes, neutral-colored furniture. There was a single, ominous box of Kleenex on the table by the couch.

When we were both settled she said, "Now. Are either of you involved with anyone outside the marriage."

I said, "You mean, like, romantically?"

Richard was already shaking his head.

"That's right," Mrs. McNabb said.

"No," Richard said.

"No," I said.

She looked at Richard for a long time, as if she didn't believe him. I didn't believe him either. "What?" he said. His arms had been folded across his chest from the moment he sat down. "I said *no,* there's nobody else."

After a few minutes she split us up. Richard waited in reception while she asked me questions. Whenever I said anything about Richard she made me preface it with "I think" or "it seems to me." I didn't mention Lili or my suspicions. Then I sat outside for half an hour, reading the same page of *Newsweek* over and over again, not able to make any sense of it.

Finally Richard came out. He was pale. "We're done," he said. "I paid her and everything."

We got in the car. Richard sat behind the wheel without starting the engine. "She asked about my parents," he said. He looked out the windshield, not at me. "I told her about how my father always made my mother bring him the mail, and then he would open it up and throw what he didn't want on the floor. And then my mother would have to get down on her knees and pick it up."

He looked so lost and childlike. I suddenly realized that the only other person who could understood what we were both going through was Richard. It was hard not to reach out for him.

"She asked me were they happy," he said. "I said no. And then the weirdest thing happened. I found myself explaining all this stuff to her. Stuff I didn't know I knew. How I'd always believed it would be so easy for my father to make my mother happy. That a marriage should work if you just didn't throw your trash on the floor for the other person to pick up. I don't remember Mrs. McNabb saying anything, it was just suddenly I had this flash of understanding. How I'd spent my life look-ing for an unhappy woman like my mother, to prove how easily I could make her happy. Only I was wrong. I couldn't make you happy after all."

That wonderful, brief moment of intimacy was gone. I was now an "unhappy woman." I didn't much like it.

"I feel all wrung out," he said, and started to cry. I couldn't remember the last time I'd seen him cry. "I don't know if I can go through this again."

"This was just the start," I said. "We haven't gotten *anywhere* yet."

He shook his head and started the car. "I don't know," he said. "I don't know if I can go on."

AND THAT was the end of counseling. The next time I brought it up Richard shook his head and refused to talk about it.

By that point he "worked late" at least two nights a week. It embarrassed me to hear the shopworn excuse. I pictured him in his office, his corduroys around his ankles, some exotic olive-skinned wanton sprawled on her back across his desk, her ankles locked behind his waist, her mouth open in an ecstatic scream, the rest of the department shaking their heads in shame as they passed his door.

I couldn't stop thinking about it. I lay awake at night and tor-tured myself. One morning in August I was so far out of my head I called Sally. "This woman Richard is supposed to be seeing. Lili or whatever her name is. Describe her."

"Can you spell slut, dear? What more do you need to know?"

"I want the details. Like you were doing it for the police."

"Oh, five-six I guess. Wavy brown hair, just to her shoulders. Deep tan. Make-up, of course. *Lots* of makeup. Did I mention arm-pit hair?"

"Yes," I said, "you did."

During summer sessions Richard taught a two-hour class, from one to three every afternoon. Assuming he was not so far gone that he'd given up teaching entirely. At one-fifteen I climbed the marble stairs to the second floor of Dallas Hall, looking for the woman Sally had described.

There was nobody in the common room. I got a cup of coffee and found Robbie in his office. "Hi," I said awkwardly. "I'm looking for one of Richard's students? Her name is Lili something? He had this paper he needed to give her and he forgot it this morning."

He didn't buy my story for a second, of course. "Ah, yes. The redoubtable Lili. She was around a while ago. I could give it to her if you wanted."

"No, that's okay. I should try to find her myself."

"Well, you can't miss her. She's only about five one, with olive skin, blonde hair to her waist, and...well, you know."

"And great tits," I said bitterly. "Right?"

Robbie shrugged, embarrassed. "You said it. Not me."

The descriptions didn't exactly match. I suspected Robbie was not seeing her with much objectivity. For that matter, neither was Sally.

The offices faced out into a central room which was divided into a maze of cubicles. I wandered through them for a while with no luck. On my way out I stopped at Taylor's secretary's office. "I'm looking for a student named Lili? She's short, with..."

"I know, the most gorgeous black hair in the world. I would hardly call her short, though—oh. There she goes right now."

I turned, hearing heels click on the polished floor. "Thanks," I said, and ran into the hall.

And froze.

She looked at me for no more than a second or two. Afterwards I couldn't say how tall she was, or describe the color of her hair. All I saw were her eyes, huge and black, like the eyes of a snake. It must have been some chemical in her sweat or her breath that I reacted to on such a blind, instinctive level. I could do nothing but stare at her with loathing and horror. When her eyes finally let me go I turned and ran all the way back to my car.

I picked Emily up at the sitter's and took her home and held her for the rest of the afternoon, until Richard arrived. I just sat there and rocked silently on the edge of the couch, remembering the blackness of those eyes, thinking, not one of us. She's not one of us.

THAT FRIDAY Richard came home at four. He was a half-hour late, no more than that. Emily was crawling furiously around the living room and I watched her with all the attention I could manage. The rest of my mind was simply numb.

Richard nodded at us and walked toward the back of the house. I heard the bathroom door close. I put Emily in her playpen and followed him. I could hear water running behind the bathroom door. Some wild bravado pushed me past my fear. I opened the door and walked in.

He stood at the sink. He had his penis in one hand and a bar of soap in the other. I could smell the sex he'd had with her, still clinging to him. The smell brought back the same revulsion I'd felt at the sight of her.

We looked at each other a long time. Finally he turned off the water and zipped himself up again. "Wash your hands," I said. "For God's sake. I don't want you touching anything in this house until you at least wash your hands."

He washed his hands and then his face. He dried himself on a hand towel and carefully put it back on the rack. He sat on the closed lid of the toilet, looked up at me, then back at the floor.

"She was lonely," he said. "I just…I couldn't help myself. I can't explain it to you any better than that."

"Lili," I said. "Why don't you say her name? Do you think I don't know?"

"Lili," he said. He got too much pleasure out of the sound of it. "At least it's out in the open now. It's almost a relief. I can talk to you about it."

"Talk to me? You *bastard!* What gives you the idea that I want to hear anything…*anything* about your cheap little slut?"

It was like he hadn't heard me. "Every time I see her she's different. She seduces me all over again. And there's this loneliness, this need in her—"

"Shut up! I don't want to hear it! Don't you care what you've done? Doesn't this marriage mean anything to you? Are you just a penis with legs? Maybe you're sick of me, but don't you care about Emily? At all?"

"I can't…I'm helpless…"

He wouldn't even offer me the dignity of putting it in past tense. "You're not helpless. You're just selfish. A selfish, irresponsible little prick." I saw myself standing there, shouting at him. It wasn't like me. It was like a fever dream. I felt weightless and terribly cold. I slammed the bathroom door on my way out. I packed a suitcase and put Emily in her carseat and carried her outside. It wasn't until we were actually moving that she started to cry.

For me it took even longer.

DARLA KNEW everything to do. She told me to finish the story while she drove me to my bank. I took all but a hundred dollars out of the checking account, and half the savings. Then she called her lawyer and set up an appointment for Monday morning. By midnight I had a one-bedroom apartment around the corner from hers. She even loaned me some Valium so I could sleep.

Even with the Valium, the first few days were hard. I would wake up every morning at five and lie there for an hour or more while my brain wandered in circles. Richard had said "Every time I see her she's different." And everyone I asked about her had a different description.

Helpless. He said he was helpless.

After a week of this I saw it wasn't going to go away. I left Emily with Darla and spent the evening at the library.

Back when I was a lab assistant, back when I first met Richard, I took English courses too. Richard was a first year teaching assistant and I was a lovestruck senior. We read Yeats and Milton and Blake and Tennyson together. And Keats, Richard's favorite.

I found the quote from Burton's *Anatomy of Melancholy* in Keats' *Selected Poetry.* "Apollonius…by some probable conjectures, found her out to be a serpent, a lamia; and that all her furniture was, like Tantalus' gold…no substance, but mere illusions." The lamia had the head and breasts of a woman and the body of a snake. She could change her appearance at will to charm any man. Like Lilith, her spiritual ancestor, she fed off the men she ensnared.

> I saw pale kings and princes too,
> Pale warriors, death pale were they all;
> They cried—"La Belle Dame sans Merci
> Hath thee in thrall!"

I drove back toward my apartment. The night was hot and still. Suppose, I thought. Suppose it's true. Suppose there *are* lamias out there. And one of them has hold of Richard.

Then, I thought, she's welcome to him.

I brought Emily home and went to bed.

BY THE SECOND WEEK it was time to look for work. With luck, and child support, I hoped to get by with a part-time job. I hated the idea of Emily in day care even half-days, but there was no alternative.

I left her at the sitter's at nine o'clock. I came back a few minutes after noon. The sitter met me at the door. She was red-faced, had been crying.

"Oh God," she said. "I didn't know where to find you."

I would stay calm, I told myself, until I found out what was wrong. "What happened?"

"I only left her alone for five minutes. We were out here in the yard. The phone rang and I went inside, and—"

"Is she hurt?" I said. I had grabbed the sitter's arms. "Is she alive? What *happened?*"

"I don't know."

"Where *is* she?"

"I don't know!" she wailed. "She just…disappeared!"

"How long ago?"

"Half an hour? Maybe less."

I turned away.

"Wait!" she said. "I called the police. They're on their way. They have to ask you some questions…"

I was already running for the car.

Subconsciously I must have made the connection. Lamia. Lilith. The legends of stolen children, bled dry, turned into vampires.

I knew exactly where Emily was.

My tires screamed as I came around the corner and again as I hit the brakes. I slammed the car door as I ran for the house. A fragment of my consciousness noticed how dead and dry the lawn looked, saw the yellowing newspapers still in their plastic wrappers. The rest of my mind could only say Emily's name over and over again.

I didn't bother with the doorbell. Richard hadn't changed the locks and the chain wasn't on the door. There were no lights inside. I smelled the faint odor of spoiled milk.

I went straight to the bedroom. The door was open.

All three of them were in there. None of them had any clothes on. Richard lay on his back. Lili crouched over him, holding Emily. The smell of spoiled milk was stronger, and the smell of sperm, and the alien sex smell, Lili's smell. There was something else, something my eyes couldn't quite make out in the darkness, something like cobwebs over the three of them.

Lili turned her head toward me. I saw the black eyes again, staring at me without fear or regret. I couldn't help but notice her body—the thick waist, the small drooping breasts.

I said, "Let go of my baby."

She pulled Emily toward her. Emily looked at me and whimpered.

I was shaking with rage. I saw a gooseneck table lamp by the bed and I grabbed it, knocking over the end table and spilling books across the floor. I swung it at Lili's head and screamed, "Let her go! Let her go!"

Lili put her arms up to protect herself, dropping Emily. I swung the lamp again and she scrambled off the bed, crouched like an animal, making no effort to cover herself.

Emily had started to cry. I snatched her up and brushed the dust or whatever it was away from her face.

"Take the child," Lili said. I had never heard her voice before. It was hoarse and whispery, but musical, like pan pipes. "But Richard is mine."

I looked at him. He seemed drugged, barely aware of what was going on around him. He hadn't shaved in days, and his eyes seemed to have sunken deep into his head. "You can have him," I said.

I backed out of the room and then turned and ran. I drove to my apartment with Emily in my arms, made myself slow down, watch the road, stop for red lights. No one followed us. "You're safe now, Tater," I told her. "Everything's going to be okay."

I bathed her and fed her and wrapped her in her blanket and held her. Eventually her crying stopped.

THE POLICE found no sign of Richard at the house. The place was deserted. I changed the locks and put it up for sale. Lili was gone too, of course. The police shook their heads when her descriptions failed to add up. Untrained observers, they said. It happened all the time. Richard and Lili would turn up, they assured me, probably at some resort hotel in Mexico. I shouldn't worry.

One night last week the phone woke me up. There was breathing on the other end. It sounded like someone fighting for air. I told myself it wasn't Richard. It was only breathing. Only a stranger, only a run-of-the-mill obscene phone call.

Some days I still wake up at five in the morning. If lamias are serpents, they can't interbreed with humans. Like vampires, they must somehow turn human children into their successors. I have no doubt that was what Lili was doing with Emily when I found her.

I can't say anything, not even to Darla. They would tell me about the stress I've been under. They would put me in a hospital somewhere. They would take Emily away from me.

She seems happy enough, most of the time. The only changes in her appearance are the normal ones for a healthy, growing baby girl. She's going to be beautiful when she grows up, a real heartbreaker. But puberty is a long way away. And I won't know until then whether or not she is still my daughter.

Time is already moving much too fast.

WILD FOR YOU

IT WAS A Pontiac Firebird with a custom paint job, a metal-flake candy-apple red. The personalized plates said WILD4U.

I was right behind her on that big clover-leaf that slopes down off Woodall Rogers onto I-35. The wind caught a hank of her long blonde hair and set it to fluttering outside her window. I saw her face in her own rear-view as she threw her head back. Laughing, or singing along with the radio, or maybe just feeling the pull as she put the pedal down and scooted into the southbound lane.

She was a beauty, all right. Just a kid, but with a crazy smile that made my heart spin.

I whipped my pickup into fourth but I couldn't get past this big white Caddy coming up on me from behind. The two lanes for Austin were fixing to split off in half a mile. An eighteen-wheeler filled up one of them and the Caddy had the other. I eased off the gas and watched her disappear over the horizon, a bright red promise of something beyond my wildest dreams.

It was mid-afternoon, sunny with a few clouds. The weather couldn't decide if it was summer or winter, which is what passes for fall in Texas. I wasn't but a kid myself, with my whole life in front of me. I put Rosanne Cash on the tape deck and my arm out the window and let those white lines fly by.

I WAS AT the Fourth Street Shell station in Waco, halfway home, when I saw that little red car again. I'd just handed my credit card to the lady when the squeal of brakes made me look up. There it was, shiny and red, rocking back and forth by the Super Unleaded.

I kept one eye on it while I signed the receipt. The driver door opened and this guy got out. He was in jeans and a pearl button shirt and a black cap. I can't say I liked the looks of him. She got out the passenger side and leaned across the top of the car, watching the traffic. I couldn't hardly see her because of the pump. I hung around the ice cream freezer, hoping she'd come inside. Instead the guy came in to pay cash for five dollars' worth.

I followed him out. She turned to get back in the car and I felt a chill. Her hair was shorter than it had been, just barely past her collar. And her face looked older too.

I couldn't figure what the hell. Maybe she'd got her hair cut? She'd had time, as fast as she'd been driving, and as long as we'd been out. I felt like I'd already spent half my life on the road. Or maybe this was her older sister had borrowed the car somehow.

Weird, is what it was. I got back in the truck and hit it on down the highway. About two miles on they came up behind me to pass, and that's when I saw the license had changed. Now it said MR&MRS.

Right as they pulled up next to me I looked over at her. She was staring out the window, right at me. She pointed a finger, like kids do when they're making a pretend pistol. And smiled, that same crooked smile.

For some reason that really got to me. I don't think I'll ever forget it.

SOME THINGS are just Mysteries, and you don't expect to understand them. When I passed that car south of Belton, there were different people in it. The woman driving looked like the blonde girl, but was old enough to be her mother. There was a dark-haired girl in the passenger seat, maybe thirty years old, and two little kids in back. The dark-haired girl was turned around to yell at them. The speed limit had gone back up to 65, but they chugged along at 60. The plates were standard Texas issue and there was bumper sticker that said ASK ME ABOUT MY GRANDBABY.

Tell the truth, I was too tired to think much of it anymore. The sun had started to set and I had this pinched kind of pain between my shoulders. About thirty miles on I saw a roadside rest stop and pulled in.

I might have slept a quarter of an hour. The sky had clouded over and the sunset lit everything up pretty spectacular. It was being thirsty woke me and I gimped over to the water fountain on stiff legs.

Luck or something made me look back at the highway. That metal-flake red Firebird pulled off at about thirty miles an hour, just barely rolling. The old lady was by herself again. While I watched she hung a left turn under the interstate and disappeared.

I had my drink of water, remembering that pointing finger and crooked smile. I got back in the pickup and followed. When I came out on the northbound access, I saw the car pulled over in the Johnson grass at the side of the road. I parked behind it and eased out of the truck.

There was nobody inside. Up ahead an ambulance screamed onto the northbound entrance ramp, siren going and lights flashing. After a few seconds the lights went out and it crested a hill, headed back the way we'd come.

STICKS

HE HAD A 12" Sony black-and-white, tuned to MTV, that sat on a chair at the end of the bed. He could barely hear it over the fan in the window. He sat in the middle of the bed because of the sag, drumming along absently to Steve Winwood's "Higher Love."

The sticks were Regal Tip 5Bs. They were thinner than 2Bs—marching band sticks—but almost as long. Over the years Stan had moved farther out over the ends. Now the butts of the sticks fit into the heels of his palms, about an inch up from the wrist. He flipped the right stick away when the phone rang.

"Stan, dude!" a voice said. "You want to work tomorrow?"

"Yeah, probably. What have you got, Darryl? You don't sound right."

"Does the name Keven Stacey mean anything to you?"

"Wait a minute." Stan switched the phone to his other ear. "Did you say Keven *Stacey*? As in Foolsgold, Kevin Stacey? She's going to record at CSR?"

"You heard me." Stan could see Darryl sitting in the control room, feet up on the console, wearing double-knit slacks and a T-shirt, sweat coming up on his balding forehead.

"This is some kind of bullshit, right? She's coming in for a jingle or a PSA."

"No bullshit, Stanley. She's cutting a track for a solo album she's going to pitch to Warner's. Not a demo, but a real, honest-to-Christ track. Probably a single. Now if you're not interested, there's plenty of other drummers in LA…"

"I'm interested. I just don't understand why she wants to fuck with a rinky-dink studio like yours. No offense."

"Don't harsh me, bud. She's hot. She's got a song and she wants to put it in the can. Everybody else is booked. You try to get into Record One or Sunset Sound. Not for six months you won't get in. Even if you're Keven Stacey. You listening, Stan?" He heard Darryl hitting the phone on the edge of the console. "That's the Big Time, dude. Knocking on your door."

JUST THE NIGHT BEFORE Stan had watched Foolsgold in concert on HBO. Everybody knew the story. Keven used to fuck the guitar player and they broke up. It was ugly and they spread it all over the *Goldrush* album. It was soap opera on vinyl and the public ate it up.

Stan too.

The set was blue-lit and smoky, so hot that the drummer looked like he'd been watered down with a garden hose. Every time the lead player snapped his head back the sweat flew off like spray from a breaking wave.

Keven stood in the middle of the stage, holding a thin white jacket around her shoulders like there was a chill in the air. When she sang she held on to the mike stand with both hands, swaying a little as the music thundered over her. Her eyes didn't go with the rest of her face, the teased yellow hair, fine as fiberglass, the thin model's nose, the carefully painted mouth. The eyes were murky and brown and looked like they were connected to brains and a sense of humor. And something else, passion and something more. A kind of conviction. It made Stan believe every word she sang.

STAN FINISHED his Dr. Pepper and went into Studio B. The rest of Darryl's first-string house band was already there, working out their nerves in a quiet, strangely frenzied jam. Stan had turned over his drums to Dr. Jackson Sax, one of the more underrated reed players in the city and a decent amateur on a trap set. Jackson's trademark was a dark suit and a pork-pie hat that made him look like a cross between a preacher and a plain-clothes cop. Stan was one of the few people he ever talked to. Nobody knew if he was crazy or just cultivating an image.

Stan himself liked to keep it simple. He was wearing a new pair of Lee riders and a long-sleeved white shirt. The shirt set off the dark skin and straight black hair he'd inherited from his half-breed Comanche father. He had two new pairs of Regal Tip 5Bs in his back pocket and white Converse All-Stars on his feet, the better to grip the pedals.

The drums were set up in a kind of elevated garden gazebo against one wall. There were boom mikes on all sides and a wooden rail across the front. If they had to they could move in wheeled walls of acoustical tile and isolate him completely from the mix. Stan leaned with his right foot up against the back wall.

There was some action in the control booth and the music staggered and died. Gregg Rosen had showed up so now everybody was looking for Keven. Rosen was her producer and also her boyfriend, if you paid attention to the gossip. Which Stan did. The glass in the booth was tinted and there was a lot of glare, but Stan could make out a Motley Crue T-shirt, purple jams, and glasses on a gold chain. Rosen's hair was crewcut on top and long enough at the sides to hit his shoulders.

They each gave Rosen some preliminary levels and then cooked for a couple of minutes. Rosen came out on the floor and moved a couple of microphones. Darryl got on the intercom from the control room and told them to shut up for a minute. He played back what he'd just taped and WhiteBread Walker, the albino keyboard player, started playing fills against the tape.

"Sounds okay," Rosen said.

"Uh, listen," Stan said. "I think the hi-hat's overmodulating."

Rosen stared at him for a good five seconds. The tape ran out and the studio got very quiet. Finally Rosen circled one finger in the air for a replay. The tape ran and then Darryl came on the speakers, "Uh, Gregg, I think the top end is, uh, breaking up a little on that hi-hat."

"Well, fix the fucking thing," Rosen said.

He walked out. As soon as the soundproof door closed there were a few low whistles and some applause. Stan leaned over until his cheek rested against the cool plastic skin of his riding tom. He could feel all the dents his sticks had left in it. Wonderful, he thought. We haven't even started and I've already pissed off the top producer in LA.

WHEN ROSEN came back Keven was with him.

Jorge Martin, the 15-year-old boy wonder, fiddled with the tailpiece on his Kramer. WhiteBread pretended to hear something wrong with the high E on his electric piano. Art, the bass player, cleaned his glasses. Stan just went ahead and stared at her, but tried to make it a nice kind of stare.

She was small. He'd known that, but the fluorescent lights made her seem terribly fragile. She wore high heeled boots, jeans rolled up tight at the cuffs, a fringe jacket and a white ribbed tank top. She looked around at the setup, nodding, working on her lower lip with her teeth. Finally her eyes met Stan's, just for a second. The rest of the room went out of focus. Stan tried to smile back at her and ended up looking down at his snare. He had a folded-up piece of newspaper duct-taped off to one side of the head to kill overtones. The tape was coming loose. He smoothed the tape with his thumbnail until he was sure she wasn't looking at him any more and he could breathe again.

"THE SONG is called 'Sticks,'" she said. She stood in front of WhiteBread's Fender Rhodes, her hands jammed nervously into her jacket pockets. "I don't have a demo or anything. Sorry. But it's pretty simple. Basically what I want is a real African sound, lots of drums, lots of backing vocals, chanting, all like that. Okay. Well, this is what it sounds like."

She started playing. Stan was disarmed by her shyness. On the other hand she was not kidding around with the piano. She had both hands on the keys and she pumped out a driving rhythm with a solid hook. She started singing. Suddenly she wasn't a skinny, shy little blonde any more. She was Keven Stacey. Everybody in the room knew it.

Stan's stomach hurt. It felt like ice had formed in there. The cold went out through his chest and down his arms and legs.

One by one they started to fall in. Stan played a roll on the hi-hat and punched accents on the kick drum. It sounded too disco but he couldn't think of anything else to play. It helped just to move his hands. After one verse Keven backed off and let WhiteBread take over the piano. She walked around and nodded and pointed, talking into people's ears.

She walked up to the drum riser and put her forearms on the railing. Stan could see the fine golden hair on her wrists. "Hi," she said. "You're Stan, right?"

"Right," he said. Somehow he kept his hands and feet moving.

"Hi, Stan. Do you think you could give me something a little more...I don't know. More primitive, or something?"

"More toms, maybe?"

"Yeah. More of a 'Not Fade Away' kind of feel."

Buddy Holly was only Stan's all-time favorite. He nodded. He couldn't seem to look away from her. His hands moved over to the toms, right crossing over left as he switched from the riding tom to the floor toms. It was a bit of flash left over from the solos he'd played back when he was a kid. He mixed it up with a half-beat of press roll here and there and let the accents float around.

"That's nice," Keven said. She was watching his eyes and not his hands. He stared back and she didn't look away.

"Thanks," he said.

"I like that a lot," she said, and flicked the side of the high tom with her fingernail. "A whole lot." She smiled again and walked away.

THE BASIC TRACK of drums, bass, and guitar went down in two takes. It was Stan's pride that they never had to put a click track on him to keep him steady. Keven and Rosen listened to the playback and nodded. Then they emptied the percussion closet. Stan put down a second drum track, just fills and punctuation, and the rest of the band loaded up another track with timbales, shakers, bongos and congas. Keven stood on top of a chair, clapping her hands over her head and moving with the music.

The tape ran out. Everybody kept playing and Rosen finally came down out of the booth to break it up, tapping on the diamond face of his Rolex. Keven got down off her chair and everything went quiet. Stan took the wing-nuts off his cymbal stands and started to pack his brass away.

"Do you sing?"

Stan looked up. Keven was leaning on the rail again, watching him.

"Yeah, a little bit. Harmonies and stuff."

"Yeah? If you're not doing anything you could stick around for a while. I could maybe use you later on."

"Sure," Stan said. "Why not?"

ROSEN WRAPPED the session at ten that night. Stan had spent five hours on hard plastic folding chairs, reading *Entertainment Weekly* and *Guitar for the Practicing Musician,* listening to WhiteBread and Jorge lay down their solos, waiting for Rosen and Keven to tinker with the mix. Keven found him there in the lounge.

"You're not doing the vocals tonight," he said.

She shook her head.

"You weren't even planning to."

"Probably not." She was smiling.

"So what am I doing here?"

"I just said I could maybe use you. I didn't say for what."

Her smile was on crooked and her shawl hung loose and open. Stan could see a small mole just below her collarbone. The skin around it was perfect, soft and golden. This isn't happening, he thought.

There was a second where he felt his life poised on a single balance point. Then he said, "You like Thai food?"

HE TOOK HER to the Siam on Ventura Boulevard. They left her car at the studio and took Stan's white CRX. The night air was cool and sweet and ZZ Top was on KLOS. The pumping, pedal-point bass and Billy Gibbon's pinched harmonics were like musk and hot sauce. Stan looked over at Keven, her hair blown back, her eyes closed, into the music. There was a stillness in the very center of Stan's being. Time had stopped.

Over dinner he told her about the sensitive singer-songwriter who'd gotten his start in junk food commercials. The guy always used pick-up musicians and then complained because they didn't know his songs. The only thing he actually took along on tour with him was his oversized white Baldwin grand piano.

The gig was in a hotel ballroom. Stan and the lead trumpet player were set up next to the piano and got to listen to his complaints through the entire first set. During the break they collected sixteen place settings of silver and laid them across the piano strings. The second set was supposed to open with "Claire de Lune" on solo piano. After the first chord the famous singer-songwriter walked off-stage and just kept walking. Stan would have lost his union card over that one, only nobody would testify against him.

Keven had done the same sort of time. After high school she'd been so broke she'd played piano in one of those red-jacket, soft-pop bands at the Hyatt Edgewater in Long Beach. When she wouldn't put out for the lead player he kept upstaging her and sticking his guitar neck in her face. One night she reached over and detuned his strings, one at a time, in the middle of his solo on "Blue Moon." The stage was so small he couldn't get away from her without falling into the first row of tables. It was the last song of the night and the audience loved it. The manager of the Hyatt wanted them to keep it in the act. Instead Keven got fired and the guitarist found another blonde piano player from LA's nearly infinite supply.

Halfway through dinner Stan felt the calf of her leg press gently against his. He returned the pressure, ever so slightly. She didn't move away.

The chopsticks fit in Stan's hands like Regal Tip 5Bs. He found himself nervously playing his empty plate and water glass. Keven put the dinner on her American Express and told him Warner's would end up paying for it eventually.

In the parking lot Stan walked her to the passenger side of his car and stopped with his hand on the door. His throat was suddenly dry and his heart had lost the beat. "Well," he said. "Where to?"

She shrugged, watched his face.

"I have a place just over on Sunshine Terrace. If you want to, you know, have a drink. Or something."

"Sure," she said. "Why not?"

SOME OF THE HOUSES around him were were multi-million dollar jobs, sprawling up and down the hillside, hidden behind trees and privacy fences. Stan had a one-bedroom apartment in a cluster of four, squeezed in between the mansions. Everything inside was wood—the paneling on the walls, the cabinets, the louvered doors and shutters. Through the open windows the cool summer wind rattled the leaves like tambourines.

Keven walked slowly around the living room, touching the shelves along the one wall that wasn't filled with windows, finally settling in an armchair and pulling her shawl around her shoulders. "I guess you're tired of people telling you how they expected to find your clothes all over the place and junk food boxes in the corners."

"People have said that, yeah."

"I'm a slob. My place looks like somebody played Tilt-A-Whirl with the rooms. And all those goddamn stuffed animals." Word had gotten out that Keven loved stuffed animals so her fans now handed them up to her by the dozen at Foolsgold concerts. "What's that?"

"It was my grandfather's," Stan said. It was the trunk of a sapling, six feet long, maybe an inch and a half in diameter at its thickest, the bark peeled away, feathers hanging off the end. Stan took it down from the wall and handed it to her. "It's a coup stick."

"Acoustic? Like a guitar?"

"Coup with a P. The Indians used it to help exterminate themselves. They thought there was more honor in touching an enemy with one of these than killing him. So they'd ride into a bunch of cavalry and poke them with their coup sticks and the cavalry would blow their heads off."

"Is that what happened to your grandfather?"

"No, he burned out his liver drinking Sterno. He was supposed to have whacked a cop with it once. All it got him was a beating and a night in jail."

"Why'd he do it?"

"Life in the big city, I guess. He had to put up with whatever people did to him and he couldn't fight back or they'd kill him. He didn't have any options under the white man's rules so he went back to the old rules. My old man said Grandpa was laughing when the cop dragged him away. You want a beer?"

She nodded and Stan brought two cans of Oly out of the kitchen. Keven was rummaging through her purse. "You want a little coke with that?" she asked.

"No thanks. You go ahead."

She cut two lines and snorted them through a short piece of plastic straw. "You're a funny kind of guy, you know that?"

"What do you mean?"

"You seem like you're just waiting for other people to catch up to you. Like you're just waiting for somebody to come up and ask you what you want. And you're ready to lay it all out for them."

"I guess maybe that's so."

"So what do you want, Stan? What you do want, right this second?"

"You really want to know? I'd like to take a shower. I really sweated it up in the studio."

"Go ahead," she said. "No, really. I'm not going anywhere. We took your car, remember?"

THE HEAT from the water went right into his muscles and he started to relax for the first time since Darryl's call the day before. And he wasn't completely surprised when he heard a tapping on the glass.

She was leaning on the sink, posed for him, when he opened the sliding door. Her hair stuck out to one side where she'd pulled her tank top over her head. Her small, soft breasts seemed to sway just a little. One smooth hip was turned toward him in a kind of unconscious modesty, not quite hiding the dark tangle of her pubic hair.

"I guess you're tired of people telling you how beautiful you are."

"Try me," she said, and got in next to him.

Her mouth was soft and enveloping. He could feel the pressure of her breasts and the small, exquisite muscles of her back as he held her. Her small hands moved over him and he thought he might pass out.

Later, in bed, she showed him what she liked, how to touch her and where. It seemed to Stan as if she'd offered him a present. She had condoms in her purse. He used his fingers and his tongue and later came inside her. She was high from the cocaine and not ready to sleep. Stan was half crazy from the touch and scent of her and never wanted to sleep again. Sometime around dawn she told him she was cold and he brought her a blanket. She curled up inside his arm, building an elaborate nest out of the pillows and covers.

They made love again in the morning. She whispered his name in his ear. Later they showered again and he made her coffee and toast.

Stan offered her one of his T-shirts but she shook her head and dressed in yesterday's clothes. Time seemed to pick up speed as she dressed. She looked at the clock and said, "Christ, it's almost noon. Gregg is going to be waiting on us."

HE STOOD in a circle with the other singers, blending his voice on an African chant that Keven had played them from a tape. He knew the gossip had started the minute he and Keven came in together. Rosen was curt and irritable and everybody seemed to watch Stan out of the corners of their eyes.

Stan couldn't have cared less.

When the backing tracks were down, Keven disappeared into the vocal booth. Jackson packed up his horn and sat down next to Stan. "Got to make a thing over at Sunset. You working this evening?"

"I don't know yet."

"Yeah," he said. "Be cool."

Rosen put the playback over the speakers. The song was about break-ups and betrayals:

> *...broke down all my fences*
> *And left me here alone*
> *Picking up sticks...*

As she stretched out the last word the percussion came up in the mix, drowning her in jungle rhythm. The weight of the drums was a perfect balance for the shallow sentiment. Together they sounded to Stan like number one with a bullet.

She nailed the vocal on the third try. When she came out of the booth she walked up to him and said, "Hey."

"Hey yourself. It's going to be a monster, you know. It's really great."

"You think so? Really?"

"Really," he said. She brushed his cheek with her hand.

"Listen," he said.

"No. I can't. I've got a dinner date with Warner's tonight. Gregg's dubbing down a cassette and we're going to play it for them. So I'm tied up until late."

"Okay," he said.

She started to walk away and then came back.

"Do you sleep with your door locked?"

HE MANAGED to fall asleep. It was an effort of will that surprised even him. When he heard the door open it was three a.m. The door closed again and he heard a slightly drunken laugh and a gentle bumping of furniture. He saw a darker shadow in the doorway of the bedroom. There was a rustle of clothing. It seemed to Stan to be the single most erotic moment of his life.

She pulled back the covers and slid on top of him. Her skin was soft and cool and rich with perfume. When she kissed him he tasted expensive alcohol on her breath.

"How were the Warner Brothers?" he whispered.

"They loved me. I'm going to be a star."

"You're already a star."

"Shhhhhh," she said.

HE OPENED HIS EYES in the morning and saw her fully dressed. "I've got to go," she said. It was only nine o'clock. "I'll call you."

It was only later that he realized the session was over. He'd never been to her place, he didn't even have a phone number where he could call her.

IT WAS LIKE he'd never had empty time to fill before. He spent most of the afternoon on the concrete stoop in front of his apartment, listening to Buddy Holly on his boombox. A mist had blown in from the Pacific and not burned off. His hands were nervous and spun his drumsticks through his fingers, over and over.

She called late that night. He should have been asleep but wasn't. There was a lot of traffic noise in the background and he had trouble hearing her. "I'll be by tomorrow night," she said. "We can go to a movie or something."

"Keven…"

"I have to go. See you tomorrow, okay?"

"Okay," Stan said.

SHE WAS SITTING on the stoop when he came home from a session the next afternoon. She was wrapped in her shawl and the clouds overhead all seemed to be in a hurry to get somewhere.

She let him kiss her, but her lips were awkward. "I can't make tonight," she said.

"Okay."

"Something came up. We'll try it another night, okay?"

"Sure," Stan said. "Why don't you give me your number?"

She stood up, took his hands as if to keep him from touching her. "I'll call you." She stopped at the gate. "I'm crazy, you know." She wouldn't look at him.

"I don't care."

"I'll call you," she said again, and ran across the street to her bright red MG. Stan held up one hand as she drove away but she didn't look back.

AFTER TWO DAYS he started to look for her. Darryl reluctantly gave him Gregg Rosen's unlisted number. Stan asked Rosen for Keven's phone number and he just laughed. "Are you crazy, or what?"

"She won't care if you give it to me. I'm the guy from the CSR session—"

"I know who you are," Rosen said, and hung up.

He left a call for her at the Warner offices in Burbank and with Foolsgold's agent. He tried all the K. Staceys in all the LA area codes.

He called Rosen again. "Look," Rosen said. "Are you stupid, or what? Do you think you're the only kid in town that's had a piece of

Keven Stacey's ass? End to end you guys would probably stretch to Tucson. Do you think she doesn't know you've been calling? Now are you going to quit hassling me or are you going to fuck over what little career you may have left?"

THE CHECK for Keven's session came in the mail. It was on CSR's account and Darryl had signed it, but there was no note in the envelope with it. On the phone Darryl said, "Face it, bud, you've been an asshole. Gregg Rosen is way pissed off. You're going to have to kick back for a while, pay some dues. Give it a couple months, maybe you can cruise back."

"Fuck you too, Darryl."

LA dried up. Stan hit the music stores and the musicians' classifieds. Most of the ads were drummers looking for work. The union offered him a six-month tour of the southern states with a revival of *Bye Bye Birdie*.

Jesus, Stan thought. Show tunes. Rednecks. Every night another Motel 6. I'm too old for this.

The phone rang.

Stan snatched it up.

"Stan. This is Dave Harris. Remember me?"

Harris was another session drummer, nothing special. He'd filled in for Stan a couple of times.

"Yeah, Dave. What's up?"

"I was, uh, I was just listening to a cassette of that Keven Stacey song? I was just wondering, like, what the hell were you doing there? I can't follow that part at all."

"What are you doing with a cassette of that song?"

"Uh oh."

"C'mon, Dave, spill it."

"They didn't tell you? Warner's going to use it as the first single from the album. So they're getting ready to shoot the video. They didn't even tell you? Oh man, that really sucks."

"Yeah, it sucks all right."

"Really Stan, I didn't know, man. I swear. They told me you couldn't make the gig."

"Yeah, okay, Dave, hang on, all right? I'm trying to figure something out, here."

STAN SHOWED UP at the Universal lot at six in the morning. He cranked down his window and smelled the dampness in the air. Birds were chattering somewhere in the distance. Stan had the pass he'd gotten from Dave Harris. He showed it to the guard and the guard gave him directions to the Jungle Lot.

A Port-A-Sign on the edge of the road marked his turnoff. Stan parked behind the other cars and vans under the palm trees. A crew in matching blue T-shirts and caps was positioning the VTRs and laying down an Astro-turf carpet for the band.

He started setting up his drums. This was as far as his imagination had been able to take him. From here on he'd have to wing it. His nerves had tunneled his vision down to the wood and plastic and chrome under his hands and he jumped when a voice behind him said, "They gonna fry your ass, boy."

Stan turned to face a six-foot-six apparition in a feathered hat, leopard scarf, chains, purple silk shirt, green leather pants, and lizard boots.

"Jackson?" Stan asked carefully.

"Something wrong?"

"Jesus Christ, man, where did you get those clothes?"

Jackson stared at him without expression. "I'm a star now. Not trash like you, boy, a *star*. Do you know who I was talking to yesterday? Bruce. That's Bruce *Springsteen*. He says he might need me for his next tour."

"That's great, Jackson. I hope it works out."

"You laugh, boy, but when Rosen see you, he gonna shit a picket fence."

Rosen, Keven, and some blond kid pulled up in a Jeep. Stan slipped deeper into the shade of a palm tree to watch. Keven and the blond kid were holding hands. The kid was dressed in a white bush jacket and Bermuda shorts. Keven was in a matching outfit that had been artfully torn and smudged by the costume crew. The blond kid said something to Keven and she laughed softly in his face.

The director called places and the rest of the band settled in behind their instruments.

"Where the fuck is the drummer?" Rosen shouted.

Stan stepped out from behind the trees.

"Oh Christ," Rosen said. "Okay, take ten everybody. You, Stan Shithead. Off the set."

Stan was looking at Keven. Say the word, he thought. Tell him I can stay.

Keven glanced at him with mild irritation and walked away. She had hold of the blond kid's hand.

Stan looked back at Rosen. A couple of grips, ex-bikers by the size of them, were headed toward him. Stan held up his hands. "Okay," he said. He put his sticks in his back pocket and pointed at his drums. "Just let me..."

"No way," Rosen said. "Leave them here. We'll get them back to you. Right now you're trespassing and I want your ass *out* of here."

On the other side of the road was a tall, grassy hill. Stan could see Keven and the blond kid halfway up it. "Okay," he said. He walked past Rosen and got in his car, started it, and got back onto the road.

Past the first switchback he pulled over and started up the other side of the hill on foot. He was still a hundred yards away from Keven when she spotted him and sent the blond kid down to cut him off.

"Don't even think about it," Stan said. The blond kid looked at Stan's face and swerved downhill toward the jungle set at a run.

"Keven!" She stopped at the top of the hill and turned back to look at him. The blond kid would be back with the bikers any minute. Stan didn't know what to say. "You're killing me," he said. "Rosen won't let me work. Did you know that?"

"Go away, Stan," she said.

"Goddammit," he said. "How was I supposed to *not* to fall in love with you? What the hell did you expect? Do you ever listen to the words of all those songs you sing?"

A hand appeared on his shoulder, spinning him around. Stan tried to duck and ended up on his back as Rosen's fist cut the air above him. No bikers then, Stan thought giddily. Not yet. He rolled a few feet, off balance. One of his drumsticks fell out of his pocket and he grabbed for it.

Rosen's looked more annoyed than anything else. "You stupid piece of shit," he said. Stan scuttled around the hillside on his palms and his ass and his feet, dodging two more wild punches. The slope made it tricky. Finally he was up again. He kept moving, letting Rosen come after him. He outweighed Rosen by at least 40 pounds and had the reach on him besides. And if he actually hit Rosen he might as well throw his drums into the Pacific. On the other hand, if he waited around long enough, the bikers might just beat him to death.

It was what his grandfather would have called a classic no-win situation.

Kill me then, Stan thought, and to hell with you. He stepped inside Rosen's next swing and tapped him, very lightly, on the chest with his drumstick. Then he stepped back, smiling, into Rosen's roundhouse left.

"HEY, SITTING BULL," a voice said. It was Keven, kneeling next to him. "I think Custer just kicked your ass."

Stan propped himself up on his elbows. He could see Rosen walking down the hill, rubbing his knuckles. "Who'd have thought the little bastard could hit so hard? Did you call him off?"

"I wasn't going to let him kill you. Even if you did deserve it." She took his face in both her hands. "Stan. What am I going to do with you?"

Stan didn't have an answer for that one.

"This doesn't change anything," she said. "It's over. It's going to stay over."

"You never called me."

She sat back, arms wrapped around herself. "Okay. I should have called. But you're a scary guy, Stan. You're just so...intense, you know? You've got so much hunger in you that it's...it's hard to be around."

Stan looked at his hands.

"I wasn't, like, just playing with you, okay? What there was, what happened, it was real. I just, I changed my mind. That's all. I'm just a person, you know. Just like anybody else."

She believed that, Stan thought, but it wasn't true. She wasn't like other people. She didn't have that fist in her stomach, pushing her, tearing up her insides. Not any more. That was what made her different, but there wasn't any point trying to tell her that.

She stood up and walked away from him, breaking into a run as she moved downhill. Rosen was there at the bottom. She took him by the arm and talked to him but Stan couldn't hear any of it. He watched the clouds for a while then headed down.

Rosen walked over, holding out his hand. "Sorry I lost my temper." Keven was back at the jungle set.

Stan took his hand. "No hard feelings."

"Keven says she wants you to do the video." Rosen clearly didn't like the idea. "She says nobody else can really do that drum part. She says there won't be any more trouble."

"No," Stan said. "No more trouble."

THE WORST PART was hearing her voice on the radio, but in time Stan even got used to that.

Her album was out just before Thanksgiving and that week they premiered the video on MTV. It opened with Keven and her boyfriend in their jungle suits, then cut back and forth between a sort of stylized Tarzan plot and the synched-up footage of the band playing under the palm trees.

The phone rang. "Dude, you watching?"

"Yeah, Darryl. I'm watching."

"Totally crucial video, bud. I'm serious."

"Good drummer," Stan said.

"The best. This is going to make your career. You are on the map."

"I could live with that. Listen, Darryl, I'll see you tomorrow, okay? I want to catch the rest of this."

Stan squatted in front of the TV. Keven sang hard into the camera. Stan could read the words of the song on her face. She turned and looked over her shoulder and the camera followed, panning past her to the drummer, a good-looking, muscular guy in his middle thirties, with black hair that hung straight to his collar. The drummer smiled at Keven and then bent back to his work.

The clear, insistent power of his drumming echoed through the jungle afternoon.

MATCH

IT WAS A good summer for tennis, hot and clear. I was newly
divorced and working at home and had my mornings free. My
partner was a radiologist from St. David's on the second shift. We
played two sets a day, three if we could take the heat.

Afternoons I cranked up the headphones and sat down at the
drawing table. I had discovered heavy metal. The louder the better—
it kept my mind on my work instead of my marriage. This week
work was one of those new fruit-juice-and-fizzy-water drinks called
Tropical Blizzards. I started sketching a layout with a sweating tennis
player. Right arm straight overhead, wrist cocked, body lunging forward. Face knotted in concentration. I worked on the face until I
could see the heat in it. Brutal heat, murderous heat.

Suddenly it was my father's face.

I saw him clutch his chest and go down. My hand started to
shake and the pencil lead snapped off.

I DIDN'T SLEEP much that night. In the morning I called my parents
in Houston and my father answered.

"It's me," I said.

"Me who?"

"It's the goddamn Easter bunny, who do you think it is?"

"My only begotten son. Big deal." From his tone of voice I was
supposed to figure he was kidding.

"I'm driving up for a meeting on Saturday. Thought I'd stay
through the weekend if that's okay."

"I don't care. Talk to your mother." The phone clunked on the table. Distantly I heard him say, "It's your son."

"Hi darling," my mother said. "How are you?"

"I'm fine, Mom. Just thought I'd come up for the weekend."

"Of course. Your room's made up and ready."

I was thirty-six. I hadn't lived with my parents in nineteen years. "I'll be in Friday afternoon. I don't know what time, so don't panic if I'm not there for dinner, okay?"

"Yes, dear," my mother said.

DINNER AT my parents' house was five p.m. sharp, in time for the evening news. I walked in as my mother set the TV tray in front of my father. Leftover pot roast, potatoes and gravy, canned green beans boiled for hours with hunks of bacon fat. I had a gray canvas bag in my left hand, with the handle of my racket sticking out.

My mother hugged me and said, "So, you're just going to let your hair grow now, is that it?" She was short, with a small pot belly and short hair dyed an odd sandy color. I got my gray hair from her. I already had more of it than my father did at sixty-eight.

"Nice to see you too, Mom."

My father squinted at me from his recliner. He wore a napkin tucked in over his shirt when he ate. He would have been six foot one, half an inch taller than me, if he ever stood up straight. He seemed to be devolving into some prototypical Texan ancestor, with long sideburns and hair combed straight back off his forehead. It made his nose seem to reach out toward his chin.

"Can you believe this crap? Thirty-two stations and not a god-damn thing worth watching."

"Great to see you too," I said.

"There's the same shitty stations you get without cable. Then there's three stations of niggers shouting at each other. Two stations of messkins. Two movie channels showing the same three movies over and over again. Rock and roll and country western on the rest. If it wasn't for sports I don't know why anybody would bother."

"Try some crack," I said. "That's how the rest of us manage."

He looked at the bag. My left hand clenched reflexively. "What's that? You're not trying to play tennis again, are you?"

"I've got a client here who plays."

"I wouldn't think it was good business to look like a jerk in front of somebody wants to give you money."

"Maybe I've been practicing."

"There's not enough practice in the world." He took a dainty bit of meat, then held the remote control out at arm's length. He switched through the channels, giving them no more than a couple of seconds each. His entire attention was on the screen.

"Is that all you brought?" my mother said, finally noticing the bag.

"I'm just staying the weekend."

"Could you two keep it down to a dull roar?" my father said. "I'm trying to watch a program here."

I MAY NOT have given much of a presentation the next morning, but I was hell on the tennis court. My client took me out to River Oaks and I slaughtered him 6-1, 6-0. As a career move, it was not exactly brilliant. I didn't care. I kept hearing my father say there wasn't enough practice in the world.

I came back to my parents' house drenched in sweat and flushed from the sun. "How'd it go?" my mother asked, meaning the presentation, of course.

I pretended to misunderstand. "Okay. My serve's a little off and I can't seem to get enough power out of my backhand."

"You're probably not swinging through," my father said, not looking up from the TV. "You always did chop your backhand."

My father had his first heart attack the summer after my junior year in high school. He was playing tennis with one of his students in 100-degree heat. My father won the first and third sets, and then he lit up a Roi-Tan cigarillo and sucked in a big lungful of smoke. He said he felt something then, like a hunger pain, so he went home and had a banana and a glass of milk. Finally he went to bed and my mother called the doctor. I remember him lying there, white and shaking. Scared, I guess. Another half hour, the doctor said, and he would have died. I used to think about that a lot.

I looked at my father and said, "Maybe I need a lesson."

"Maybe you do."

My mother said to him, "You can't go on a tennis court. It would kill you."

"Says who?"

"Says Dr. Clarendon."

"It's not going to kill me to go out and look at his backhand."

My mother turned to me. The look said don't let him do this. If you let him do this I'll never forgive you.

I thought about the time I ran away from home. It was the year after his heart attack. My mother promised we'd get counseling, talked me into coming back. The counselor turned out to be Dr. Clarendon. Mom took my father's side, and lied to protect him. Funny how things like that can still jerk your emotions around, even after twenty years.

I looked at my father. "Great," I said. "We'll go out tomorrow morning."

I LAY AWAKE past midnight in the tiny twin bed. Finally I told myself I wouldn't go through with it. I'd let the old man coach me a little and we'd come home. It bought me a few hours' sleep.

My father looked ten years younger Sunday morning. He wore his plain white tennis shorts and T-shirt to the breakfast table. Only queers, of course, wore all those bright colored outfits. He leaned forward and slurped loudly at his Shredded Wheat. "You're not dressed yet," he said.

"My stuff is in the wash." I'd brought blue shorts and a red T-shirt, just to stimulate his blood pressure.

"I thought we were playing this *morning*." My father had been compulsively early all his life. If I said nine o'clock, he was impatient and angry by eight-thirty.

"Let your breakfast settle," I said. I couldn't eat. I choked down some orange juice and felt it eat through my stomach lining.

I kept him waiting until ten. The temperature was already in the 80s and the air was like wet cotton. I drove us out to the courts we'd used when I was at Rice. They had fabric nets and a good composite surface, green inside the baselines and brick red outside. Pine trees grew right up to the fence and dropped their needles on the back-court. I could smell pine sap baking in the heat.

I got a bucket of tennis balls out of the trunk. "Haven't you got anything but those goddamn green balls?" My father was headed for the far court, working his arm in a circle. He had an ancient Jack Kramer wood racket, still in the press.

I carried the bucket to the other baseline. "They don't make white balls anymore. They haven't for ten years. You might as well forget about it."

"TV made them do that. You can't see a green ball as well as a white one." He threw the racket press aside, slashed the air with the racket. "You've got no depth perception on it. All it does is show up better on a TV screen."

"The players like them better. The human eye sees green better than any other color. Scientific fact."

"Bullshit. Don't tell me about science. What do you know about science?"

My father was a structural engineer. He worked on survey teams all through high school in the 30s. He laid the course for I-35 all the way from Dilley, where his mother grew up, to the Mexican border. He joined the corps to get free tuition at A&M's engineering school, and when the beatings and hazing got too bad he convinced a maiden aunt to send him to UCLA. He was a self-made man, the son of dirt-poor Texas farmers, and he'd fought his way up to a tenured professorship at Rice University. He tended to not let anyone forget it.

I rubbed sunscreen on my arms and legs, then put sweatbands on my head and wrists. My father wolf-whistled. "Hey, bathing beauty. Any time you want to play some tennis."

I took two balls out of the bucket. I shoved one in my left pock-et and squinted across the court. I was so pissed off I could feel it like something sharp stuck in my throat. I served at my father as hard as I could.

He stepped out of the way and said, "You still serve like a girl. Get that toss higher."

I REMEMBERED playing canasta with my father as a child, his smearing the cards together on the table because I was beating him, the cards bending and tearing, me starting to cry in helpless rage.

I tried to serve like a precision robot, hating myself because I didn't just walk away. My father crouched inside his baseline, leaning theatrically from side to side, swatting my serves long or into the net, not trying for the ones that were out of reach. After every serve he would point out what I did wrong, over and over, in a bored voice.

The bucket was empty. I started to gather up the balls. My father could have helped, but instead he watched, smiling sarcastically. I was painfully aware of my ass sticking out as I bent over. We traded sides and I picked up the rest of the balls. I stood on the baseline with the bucket next to my feet.

We'd played doubles with his students here, every playable Sunday, no matter how tired or hungover I was. I'd learned to pray for rain. My father had recovered from the heart attack and promised my mother he wouldn't overdo. I remembered the way he gloated over every point we won, and rode home in brooding silence if we lost.

"Waiting for something?" my father asked.

I bounced the ball with my left hand. It was the same motion as the toss, except the opposite direction. The idea was to focus on it. I couldn't focus. All I could hear was my heart, beating like crazy. I want it, I thought. I want it now.

"How about a game?" I said.

"Don't make me laugh. I can still kick your ass, on or off the court."

Twenty years ago, just out of the hospital, he'd said the same thing. He hadn't even made it into the house yet. He stood wobbling in the driveway, weak, gray-skinned, barely able to walk, threatening to kick my ass. Just the memory of it made my breath come fast.

"Prove it, old man."

I'd never said anything like it before, not to anybody. I felt the racket shiver in my hand.

"Serve 'em up," my father said. The look in his eyes was final. I'd done something that couldn't be undone. I felt like I was on a deserted stretch of interstate with the pedal all the way to the floor.

I picked out three balls and carried the bucket to the side of the court. I rolled one ball back to the chain link fence, put one in my left hand pocket. I leaned forward, bouncing the third in front of me.

I tossed the ball for the serve. My hand shook and the ball curved back over my head. I swung at it anyway and hit it into the net.

My father took one step closer.

I tried to get my breathing to even out. I couldn't get my breath at all. I took the second ball out of my pocket and bounced it, thinking, relax, relax. I pressed the ball into the racket head as I started my backswing. It felt all wrong. The toss was too low and I hit into the net again.

Double fault. My father straightened up and walked over to the ad court. I went to the net and picked the balls up, slapping the second with the racket so I could snag it out of the air. It got away from me. I chased after it, feeling my father's eyes on me the whole time.

"Love fifteen," I said. I pictured the serve in my mind and took a practice swing. I tossed the ball and hit it long.

"Back," my father said.

I was a little kid again, ugly, clumsy, with patches on my jeans and silver caps on my front teeth. I hated that little kid with everything I had. I got out the second ball and made a perfect, unselfconscious swing. The ball hit inside the line on my father's backhand. He jumped at it, took a stiff swing, and knocked it into the fence behind me.

I collected the balls and moved to the deuce court. "Fifteen all," I said. The first serve went in and my father hit it sharply down the backhand line. I got to and hit it crosscourt, thinking, run, you bastard, run. He stretched to make it, his shoes squealing as he turned. The ball floated back to me like a wounded bird. I hit it deep to his forehand. He chased it and didn't get there in time.

The knot in my guts loosened and the piney air tasted sweet and cool. I aced the next point and on the next my father hit into the net. It was my game. We changed sides and I put the balls on my father's outstretched racket.

The sun started to bear down. There were only a couple of dry places on my father's shirt, high on his chest. "Think you can serve?" I asked. The doctors took a lump out of his lung five years ago and he still complained about the pain in his shoulder muscles.

"Good enough for you," he said.

He took a few practices. His backswing had a hitch in it and he couldn't get any height or power. The few balls that got over had no pace. My father saw where the serves hit and got a look in his eyes that I'd only seen once before. It was after his second heart attack, when they brought him into the ICU. He had an oxygen tube up one nostril and a catheter coming out from under the sheet. My mother said, "Well, dear, you're just going to have to take it a little easier." My father looked like a dying shark, hanging from the scales, eyes bitter and black and empty.

"Listen," I said. "We don't need to do this." It hurt me to look at him. All I could think of was my mother, what she would say. "C'mon. Let's go home, get something to drink."

"No. You've got this coming to you." He served, and I saw him wince from the pain. The ball came in soft and I moved up on it automatically, driving it hard and deep to his backhand. He ran for it, missed, and went down on all fours.

I started for him. He got up into a crouch and froze me with a look. "Get away," he said. He picked up the ball and got ready to serve again. "Love fifteen," he said.

HE LASTED five games, and lost every one. I gave up trying to stop it. He was clearly exhausted, could hardly chase the ball. But he would not quit.

He started the sixth game with a junk serve, the ball flipped head-high and cut with exaggerated spin. I couldn't do anything with it. I hit it into the net, and the one after it into the fence. The third I couldn't even reach.

I moved up to the service line. "Forty love," my father said. "Set point."

I stared at him. Was he crazy? If he took this point he would win his first game of the day. If *I'd* been ahead forty love, *then* it would have been set point, set point for *me*. Did he not even know the difference?

He started to toss the ball. It dropped at his feet and rolled away. Then the racket came out of his hand and clattered on the court. His face was the color of wet cement. He put his hands on his hips and stood there, looking down, fighting for breath.

"Dad?" I said. But I already knew what had happened. Here it is, I thought. You did it. You killed him. Just like you always wanted. I took two steps toward him.

"Get away," my father said. He picked up the racket. I could hear his scratchy breathing all the way across the court. "Get away, goddamn you." He picked up a ball and hit it into the empty court before I could get to him. "Game," he said. "Set, match, and tournament."

He staggered to the fence and started to put the brace on his racket.

"Dad! Dad, goddammit!"

He looked at me. "What?"

"You're having a heart attack. Will you get in the goddamn car? I'm taking you to the hospital."

"Shit. Heart attack. What do you know about heart attacks?" He picked up the bucket and waited by the trunk until I unlocked it for him. He put the bucket and the rackets inside and slammed it closed. I watched him walk around the car and open his door and get in. He could barely move his feet, barely shut the door.

I got in and said, "I'm taking you to the hospital."

"You're taking me home. If you even start toward the hospital I'll open this door and get out, no matter how fast you're going. You hear me?"

He was sitting up straight, calm, one arm stuck out the window, the other on the back of the seat. Except for the fact that there was no color in his face he looked completely normal.

I knew what I'd seen. His heart had gone into fibrillation and he'd choked it down and ridden it out.

I drove him home.

When we got there he went straight to the bedroom. I heard the shower start up.

"Is he all right?" my mother asked.

"No. I think he had a heart attack."

My mother squeezed her mouth into a hard, straight line. "You couldn't stop him."

"No. This isn't...I didn't want this to happen."

"If he dies—he dies. I guess." It was the kind of thing she always said, to convince herself she didn't care.

I went to my room and packed my bag. When I came out my father was sitting in front of the TV, shouting at my mother. "I'm not going to the fucking hospital. Now go away and leave me alone."

My mother walked me out to the car. She was crying. I put my arms around her. I wished I could cry too. I wished it was that simple. "I'll call you," I said, and got in the car.

IT WAS A two-hour drive to Austin. After a while I couldn't think about my father anymore and then I was thinking about my ex-wife. Counseling hadn't been able to save the marriage. We found ways to blame each other for everything—bounced checks, bad sex, spoiled food in the refrigerator.

When I was in grade school my smart mouth was my only defense. I was no good at sports and worthless in a fight, but I could hurt people with words. I never learned to stop. Even when the thing that had saved me in grade school began to kill my marriage.

I thought of the strength it would take to fight off a heart attack. It was the same kind of strength it took to pull yourself off a shit-poor Texas farm and become a professor at a major university, with two cars and a big house and a cabinet full of French wines. A strength that didn't know when to stop.

THE FIRST THING I saw when I got home was the sketch of the tennis player. His face was intent, unforgiving. I tore it up and threw it away.

When I got out of the shower the pain was still there, knotted up in my stomach. I taped a sheet of clean, white bristol board to the drafting table. I looked at it for a long time, trying to see what was inside it, waiting for me. After a while I started to draw.

It was a young woman in a sundress, someone I'd never seen before. She walked barefoot down a beach. She was thirsty. She licked her lips. She saw something in the distance and smiled. Maybe it was a bottle of my client's fruit drink. Seagulls drifted overhead, riding the updraft in the hot afternoon.

Oz

THEY FUCKING ripped the joint. Ozzie bit the head off a white lab rat during "CIA Killers" and Toad threw a 16-inch floor tom into the audience. Three girls rushed Ozzie during "Bay of Piggies," one of them with no shirt on. The cops had to empty the place with tear gas.

The goddamn reporters were mobbed outside. "Twenty-five years," one of them shouted. "How does it feel?"

"Piss off," Ozzie said. He was pushing fifty, still skinny and barely strong enough to last through a two-hour set. How the hell was he supposed to feel? "I was acquitted, remember? You know who did it. They all went to jail. All hundred and fifty of them. So leave me the fuck alone."

"But why rock and roll?" another one shouted.

Because I was going nuts. Framed, beaten, tried, but never forgiven. Fuck you all, he thought. You got the greatest era of peace in the history of the world. No more assassinations, America out of Vietnam before it even got ugly, manned colonies on Mars. All because one reporter stumbled on the biggest conspiracy in history, with agents everywhere from the Mafia to the CIA to the Birchers to the goddamn Rosicrucians. All of them in Attica now, the ones that had lived.

But what about me?

"Why not?" Ozzie said.

"Lee!" another one shouted. "Lee, over here!"

"It's not Lee any more," Ozzie snarled. "It's Ozzie Oswald, nice and legal, got it?"

Then he was into the limousine, soundproof, bulletproof, the kind Kennedy should have had. He laughed at the crowd and held up his middle fingers. If I had it to do over, he thought, I *would* have killed him myself. What do you think about that?

The limo took him off, laughing, into the night.

GOLD

PIRATE GOLD. Coins, rings, ingots. Necklaces of emeralds and opals and sapphires. Chalices, bracelets, daggers inlaid with diamonds and lapis and ivory.

Malone rolled over in the soft hotel bed.

Not just gold but the things it would buy. A two-story house of brick and wrought iron. Greek columns in front and coaches parked in the drive. Built high on the center of Galveston Island, away from the deadly storms of the Gulf, away from the noise and stink of the port. White servants and negro slaves. Fair-haired women to sit at the piano in his parlor. Dark-skinned women to open their legs to him in the secrecy of the night…

He sat up in a sweat. I will think no evil thoughts, he told himself.

Outside, the sun rose over New Orleans. Horse-drawn carts creaked and rattled through the streets, and chickens complained about the light. The smell of the Mississippi, damp and sexual, floated through the open window.

Malone got up and put a robe on over his nightshirt, despite the heat. He turned up the gas lamp over the desk, took out pen, ink and paper, and began to write.

"My dearest Becky…"

HE SMELLED the French Market before he saw it, a mixture of decayed fruit, coffee, and leather. He crossed Decatur Street to avoid a side of beef hung over the sidewalk, swarming with flies. Voices shouted in a dozen different languages. All manner of decrepit wooden carts stood on the street, their contents passed from hand to hand until they disappeared under the yellow canvas awnings of the market. Beyond the levee Malone could see the tops of the masts of the tall ships that moved toward the Governor Nicholl's Street Wharf.

The market was crowded with cooks from the town's better families, most of them Negro or Creole. The women wore calico dresses and aprons and kerchiefs, in all shades of reds and yellows and blues. The men wore second-hand suits in ruby or deep green, with no collars or neckties. Like their suits, their hats were battered and several years out of style. They carried shopping baskets on their shoulders or heads because there was no room to carry them at their sides.

Malone let himself be drawn in. He moved slowly past makeshift stands built of crates and loose boards, past heaps of tomatoes and peppers and bananas and field peas, searching the faces of the vendors. His concern turned out to be groundless; he recognized Chighizola immediately.

Nez Coupe, Lafitte had called him. With the end of his nose gone, he looked like a rat that stood on hind legs, sniffing at something foul. The rest of his ancient face was covered with scars as well. One of them, just under his right eye, looked pink and newly healed. He was tiny, well over eighty years old now, his frock coat hanging loose on his shoulders. Still his eyes had a fierce look and he moved with no sign of stiffness. His hands were large and energetic, seeming to carry his arms unwillingly behind them wherever they went.

"Louis Chighizola," Malone called out. The old man turned to look at him. Chighizola's eyes were glittering black. He seemed ready to laugh or fly into a rage at a moment's notice. Malone pushed closer. "I need a word with you."

"What you want, you?"

"I have a proposition. A business proposition."

"This not some damn trash about Lafitte again?" The black eyes had narrowed. Malone took a half step back, colliding with an enormous Negro woman. He no longer doubted that some of Chighizola's scars were fresh.

"This is different, I assure you."

"How you mean different?"

"I have seen him. Alive and well, not two weeks ago."

"I got no time for ghosts. You buy some fruit, or you move along."

"He gave me this," Malone said. He took a flintlock pistol from his coat, holding it by the barrel, and passed it to the old man.

Chighizola looked behind him, took one reluctant step toward Malone. He took the pistol and held it away from him, into the sunlight. "Fucking hell," Chighizola said. He turned back to Malone. "We talk."

CHIGHIZOLA LED HIM east on Chartres Street, then turned into an alley. It opened on a square full of potted palms and flowers and sheets hung out to dry. They climbed a wrought-iron spiral staircase to a balcony cluttered with pots, old newspapers, empty barrels. Chighizola knocked at the third door and a young woman opened it.

She was an octoroon with skin the color of Lafitte's buried gold. She wore a white cotton shift with nothing under it. The cotton had turned translucent where it had drunk the sweat from her skin. Smells of fruit and flowers and musk drifted from the room behind her.

Malone followed the old man into an aging parlor. Dark flowered wallpaper showed stains and loose threads at the seams. A sofa with a splinted leg sat along one wall and a few unmatched chairs stood nearby. An engraving of a sailing ship, unframed, was tacked to one wall. Half a dozen children played on the threadbare carpet, aged from a few months to six or seven years. Chighizola pointed to a chair and Malone sat down.

"So. Where you get this damn pistol?"

"From Lafitte himself."

"Lafitte is dead. He disappears thirty years ago. The Indians down in Yucatan, they cook him and eat him I think."

"Is the pistol Lafitte's, or is it not?"

"You are not Lafitte, yet *you* have his pistol. Any man could."

Malone closed his eyes, fatigue taking the heart out of him. "Perhaps you are right. Perhaps I have only deceived myself." A small child, no more than two years old, crawled into Malone's lap. She had the features of the woman who answered the door, in miniature. Her dress was clean, if too small, and her black hair had been pulled back and neatly tied in red and blue ribbons. She rubbed the wool of Malone's coat, then stuck two fingers in her mouth.

"I do not understand," Chighizola said. "You come to me with this story. Do you not believe it yourself?"

"I wish I knew," Malone said.

MALONE WAS BORN poor in Ohio. His parents moved to the Republic of Texas in 1837 to get a new start. Some perverse symbolism made them choose the island of Galveston, recently swept clean by a hurricane. There they helped with the rebuilding, and Malone's father got work as a carpenter. Malone was ten years old at the time, and the memories of the disaster would stay with him the rest of his life. Block-long heaps of shattered lumber, shuffled like cards, the ruin of one house indistinguishable from the next. Stacks of bodies towed out to sea, and those same bodies washing in again days and weeks later. Scuff marks six feet up inside one of the few houses left standing, where floating furniture had knocked against the walls. The poor, Malone saw, would always be victims. For the rich there were options.

One of the richest men on Galveston Island was Samuel May Williams. On New Year's Day of 1848 he had opened the doors of the Commercial and Agricultural Bank of Texas, his lifetime dream. It sat on a choice piece of land just two blocks off the Strand Avenue, "the Wall Street of Texas." Williams' fellow Texans hated him for his shrewd land speculation, his introduction of paper money to the state, his participation in the corrupt Monclova legislature of '35. Malone thought them naive. Williams was a survivor, that was all.

Not like his father, who found that a new start did not necessarily mean a new life. Malone's mother died, along with a quarter of Galveston's population, in the yellow fever epidemic of '39. Soon his father was drinking again. Between the liquor and his son's education, there was barely money for food. Malone swore that he would see his father in a fine house in the Silk Stocking district. He never got the chance. Instead he returned from Baylor University in the spring of '48 in time to carry one corner of his father's coffin.

Malone's classes in accounting were enough to land him a position as a clerk in Sam Williams' new bank. Within a year he had married the daughter of one of its board members. His father-in-law made Malone a junior officer and an acceptable member of society. A long, slow climb lay ahead of him, leading to a comfortable income at best. It did not seem enough, somehow.

He had been in Austin on the bank's business. It was a foreclosure, the least pleasant of Malone's duties. The parcel of land was one that Williams had acquired in his early days in Texas, "going halves" with immigrants brought in by the Mexican government.

That night he had stood at the Crystal Saloon on Austin's notorious Congress Avenue, drinking away the sight of the sheriff examining Malone's papers, saying, "Sam Williams, eh?" and spitting in the dirt, the sight of the Mexican family disappearing on a mule cart that held every battered thing they owned.

A tall man in a bright yellow suit had stood at Malone's table, nodded at his satchel, and said, "On the road, are you?" The man spat tobacco onto the floor, the reason Malone had kept his satchel safely out of the way. The habit was so pervasive that Malone took precautions now by instinct. "I travel myself," the man said. "I am in ladies' garments. By trade, that is."

Malone saw that it was meant to be a joke. The drummer's name was O'Roarke, but he constantly referred to himself in the third person as Brimstone Jack, "on account of this head of hair." He lifted his hat to demonstrate. The hair that was visible was somewhere between yellow and red, matching his mustache and extravagant side-whiskers. There was, however, not much of it.

Malone mentioned Galveston. The talk soon turned to Jean Lafitte, the world's last pirate and the first white settler of Galveston Island. That was when O'Roarke offered to produce the genuine article.

Four glasses of bourbon whiskey had raised Malone's credulity to new heights. He followed O'Roarke to a house on West Avenue, the limits of civilization, and there stepped into a world he had never seen before. Chinese, colored, and white men sat in the same room together, most of them on folding cots along the walls. Heavy, sour smoke hung in the air. The aroma left Malone both nervous and oddly euphoric. "Sir," he said to O'Roarke, "this is an opium den."

A man in the far corner began to laugh. The laugh went on and on, rich, comfortable, full of real pleasure. Malone, his good manners finally giving way to curiosity, turned and stared.

The laughing man had fair skin, a hatchet nose, and piercing black eyes. His black hair fell in curls to the middle of his back. He was in shirt sleeves, leather trousers, and Mexican sandals. There was a power about him. Malone felt a sudden, strong desire for the man's good opinion.

"May I present," O'Roarke said with a small bow, "the pirate Jean Lafitte?"

Malone stared in open disbelief.

"Privateer," the dark-haired man said, still smiling. "Never a pirate."

"Tell him," O'Roarke said to the dark-haired man. "Tell him who you are."

"My name is John Lafflin," the man said.

"Your real name," O'Roarke said, "damn you."

"I have been known by others. You may call me Jean Lafitte, if it pleases you."

"Lafitte's son, perhaps," Malone said. "Lafitte himself would be, what, nearly seventy years old now. If he lived."

The hatchet-faced man laughed again. "You may believe me or not. It makes no difference to me."

SITTING THERE in Chighizola's apartment, watching dust motes in the morning sunlight, Malone found his own story more difficult to believe than ever. From the shadows the woman watched him in silence. He wondered how foolish he must look to her.

"And yet," Chighizola said, "you *did* believe him."

"It was something in his bearing," Malone said. "That and the fact that he wanted nothing from me. Not even my belief. I found myself unable to sleep that night. I returned to the house before dawn and searched his belongings for evidence."

"Which is when you stole the pistol. He did not give it to you."

"No. He had no desire to convince me."

"So why does this matter so much to you?"

Malone sighed. Sooner or later it had to come out. "Because of the treasure. If he is truly Lafitte—or even if he is merely Lafitte's son—he could lead us to the treasure."

"Always to the treasure it comes."

"I grew up on Galveston Island. We all live in the shadow of Jean Lafitte. As children we would steal away into the bayous and search for his treasure. Once there we found grown men doing the same. And if I feel so personally connected, how can you not feel even more so? It is your treasure as much as Lafitte's. You sailed with him, risked your life for him. And yet look at yourself. In poverty, living by the labor of your hands."

"I have not much time left."

"All the more reason you should want what is yours. You should want the money for your family, for your daughter here, and her children."

Chighizola looked at the woman. "He thinks you are my daughter, him." She came over to kiss his scarred and twisted face. Malone felt his own face go red. "Here is a boy who knows nothing of life."

"I am young," Malone said. "It is true. But so is this nation. Like this nation I am also ambitious. I want more than my own enrichment. I know that it takes money to bring about change, to create the growth that will bring prosperity to everyone."

"You sound like a politician."

"With enough money, I would become one. Perhaps a good one. But without your help it will never happen."

"Why am I so important? This man, Lafitte or not, what does it matter if he can lead you to the treasure?"

"If he is Lafitte, he will listen to you. He cares nothing for me. He will lead me nowhere. I need you to make him care."

"I will think on this."

"I am stopping at the French Market Inn. My ship leaves tomorrow afternoon for Galveston. I must know your answer by then."

"Tell me, you who are in such a hurry. What of ghosts?"

"I do not understand."

"Ghosts. The spirits of the dead."

"Lafitte is alive. That is all that concerns me."

"Ah, but you seek his gold. And where there is gold, there are ghosts. Always."

"Then I leave them to you, old man. I will take my chances with the living."

MALONE HAD ALREADY packed his trunk and sent for his bill when the woman arrived. He mistook her knock for the bellman and was shocked into silence when he opened the door. Finally he backed away and stammered an apology.

"I bring a message from Chighizola," she said. She pushed the door closed and leaned her weight against it. "We will go with you to see this Lafitte."

"'We?'" Malone could not take his eyes away from her.

"He says we are to divide the treasure four ways, equal shares, you, me, Louis, Lafitte."

"Which leaves the two of you with half the treasure. I thought he did not care for money."

"Perhaps not. Perhaps you care too much for it."

"I am not a schoolboy. I have no desire to be taught humility at Chighizola's hands."

"Those are his terms. If they are agreeable, we leave today."

Malone took a step closer to her. Curls of black hair had stuck to the damp flesh of her throat. It was difficult for him to speak. "I do not know your name."

"Fabienne."

"And what is your interest in this?"

"Louis," she said. "He is my only interest." She stepped to one side and pulled the door open. "We will meet you at the wharf in one hour." She closed the door behind her.

THE VOYAGE TO Galveston took a day and a half aboard the S.S. Columbia, now-aging stalwart of the Morgan line. Malone saw Chighizola and his woman only once, when the three of them shared a table for dinner. Otherwise Malone remained in his cabin, catching up on accounts and correspondence.

Malone stood on the bow as the ship steamed into Galveston Bay. Even now Sam Williams might have his eye on him. Legend had it that Williams watched incoming ships with a telescope from the cupola of his house, deducing their cargoes from their semaphored messages. He would then hurry into town to corner the market on the incoming merchandise. It did not increase his popularity. Then again, Williams had never seen public opinion as a necessary condition for money and power.

Williams had proven what a man of ambition could do. He had arrived in Texas under an assumed name in May of 1822, fleeing debts as so many others had. He had created himself from scratch. Malone knew that he could do the same. It was not proper that a man should live on his wife's fortune and social position. He needed to increase and acquire, to shape the world around him.

Chighizola joined him as they swung in toward the harbor. "Do you never miss the sea?" Malone asked him.

"I had enough of her," Chighizola said. "She care for nobody. You spend your life on top of her, she love you no more than she did the first day. A woman is better." He squinted at the island. The harbor was crowded with sailboats and steamers, and beyond it the two-story frame buildings of the Strand were clearly visible. "Hard to believe that is the same Campeachy." He looked at Malone. "Galveston, you call it now. Are there still the snakes?"

"Not like there used to be."

"Progress. Well, I will be glad to see it. Every new thing, it always is such a surprise for me."

"You will have to see it another time. We must catch a steamer for the mainland this morning, then a coach to Austin."

"Yes, I forget the hurry you are in."

"I have to know. I have to know if it is Lafitte or not."

"It is him."

"How can you be certain without even seeing him? I tell you he looks no more than forty years old."

"And I tell you we buried Lafitte twice, once at the Barataria, once at Campeachy."

"Buried him?"

"For being dead. Lafitte, he eats the blowfish, him. You understand? Poison fish. In Haiti he learns this. Sometimes he eats it, nothing happens. Sometimes he loses the feeling in his tongue, his mouth. Twice he gets stiff all over and looks dead. Twice we bury him, twice the Haitian spirit man watch the grave and dig him up again. Ten years he eats the blowfish, that I know him. In all that time, he gets no older. But it makes him different, in his head. Money is nothing to him after. Then the second time, he cares about nothing at all. Sets fire to Campeachy, sails off to Yucatan with his brother Pierre."

"I have read the accounts," Malone said. "Lt. Kearny and the *Enterprise* drove him away."

"You think one man, one ship, stand against Lafitte if he wants to fight? He sees the future that night. He sees more and more Lt. Kearnys in their uniforms, with their laws and courts and papers. More civilization, like in Louisiana. More government telling you what you can do. No more room for privateers. No place left in this country where a man stands alone. So he goes to Mexico. But first, before he goes, we burn the whole town to the ground. So Lt. Kearny does not get Lafitte's nice red house."

Malone knew that Lafitte's pirate camp had numbered two thousand souls by the time Kearny arrived in 1821. Lafitte himself ruled from a two-story red house near the port, surrounded by a moat, guarded by his most loyal men. Campeachy had been a den of vice and iniquity: gaming, whores, liquor, gun-fights and duels. There were those in Galveston still that wondered if the island would ever recover from the evil that had been done there.

Malone shook his head. Chighizola had got him thinking of ghosts and now he could not rid himself of them.

"You did not go with him," Malone said. "To Mexico. Why not?"

"I do not like the odds. I think, a man looks at Death so many times, then one day Death looks back. Life always seems good to me. I am not like Lafitte, *moi*. I do not have these ideas and beliefs to keep me awake all night. You are still young, I give you advice. To sleep good at night, this is not such a bad thing."

THE COACH took them from Houston to San Felipe along the Lower Road, then overland to Columbus. From there along the Colorado River to La Grange and Bastrop and Austin. Chighizola was exhausted by the trip, and the woman Fabienne blamed Malone for it. Malone was tired and irritable himself. Still he forced himself out of the hotel that night to search for Lafitte.

The opium house was deserted, with no sign left of its former use. He stopped in two or three saloons and left word for O'Roarke, then gave up and retired to the comparative luxury of the Avenue Hotel.

Malone searched all the next day, asking for both O'Roarke and Lafitte by name. The first name met with shrugs, the second with laughter. Malone ordered a cold supper sent to his room, where he ate in silence with Chighizola and the woman.

"It would seem," the woman said, "that we have come a long, painful distance for nothing." She was dressed somewhat more formally than Malone had seen her before, in a low-cut yellow frock and a lace cap. The dangling strings of the cap and her dark, flashing eyes made her seem as wanton as ever.

"I do not believe that," Malone said. "Men have destinies, just as nations do. I cannot believe that my opportunity has passed me by."

There was a knock and Malone stood up. "That may be destiny even now."

It was in fact O'Roarke, with Lafitte in tow. "I heard," O'Roarke said, "you sought for Brimstone Jack. He has answered your summons." He noticed Fabienne, removed his hat, and directed his gobbet of tobacco juice at the cuspidor rather than the floor.

Malone turned back to the room. Chighizola was on his feet, one hand to his throat. "Holy Christ," he said, and crossed himself.

Lafitte sank into an armchair. He seemed intoxicated, unable to focus his eyes. "Nez Coupe? Is it really you?"

"Me, I look how I should. You are the one that is not to be believed. Lafitte's son, you could be."

Malone said, "I warned you."

"A test," Chighizola said. "That is what you want, no?"

Malone shrugged. "I feel certain it would reassure us all."

Chighizola rubbed a thick scar that ran along the edge of his jaw. "There is a business with a golden thimble I could ask him about."

Lafitte waved his hand, bored. "Yes, yes, of course I remember the thimble. But I suppose I must tell the story, to satisfy your friends." He shifted in the chair and picked at something on his shirt. "It happened in the Barataria. We had made the division of the spoils from a galleon taken out in the Gulf. There were three gold coins left over. I tried to give them to your wife." His eyes moved to Fabienne, then back. "Your wife of the time, of course. But you were greedy and wanted them for yourself. So I had the smith make them into a thimble for her. I think it ended up in a chest full of things that we buried somewhere."

"It is Lafitte," Chighizola said to Malone. "If you doubted it."

"No," Malone said, "I had no doubt." He turned to O'Roarke. "How can we reward you for bringing him to us?"

"You can cut me in on the treasure," O'Roarke said. Lafitte put back his head and laughed.

"I do not know what you mean," Malone said.

O'Roarke's face became red. "Do not take Brimstone Jack for an idiot. What you want is obvious. You are not the first to try. If you succeed I would ask for only a modest amount. Say, a hundredth share. It would be simpler to cut me in than to do the things you would have to do to lose me."

Malone looked at Chighizola. Chighizola said, "It comes from your share, not from ours." Fabienne smiled her agreement.

"All right, damn it," Malone said. "Done."

Lafitte leaned forward. "You seem to have matters well in hand. Perhaps I should be on my way."

Malone stared at him for a second in shock. "Please. Wait."

"You, sir, though I know your face, I do not know your name. I seem to remember you in connection with the disappearance of my pistol."

Malone handed the pistol to Lafitte, butt first. With some embarrassment he said, "The name is Malone."

"Mr. Malone, now that you have divided up my treasure, may I ask a question or two? How do you know the treasure even exists? If it does exist, that I have not long ago spent it? If I have not spent it, that I even recall where it was buried?" Unspoken was the final question: if he recalled it, why should he share?

"Is there a treasure?" Malone asked at last.

Lafitte took out a clay pipe shaped like some Mexican deity and stuffed it with brittle green leaves. He did not offer the odd tobacco to anyone else. When he lit it the fumes were sour and spicy. Lafitte held the smoke in his lungs for several long seconds then exhaled loudly. "Yes, I suppose there is."

"And you could find it again?"

Lafitte shrugged again. "Perhaps."

"You make sport of us, sir. You know our interests, and you seem to take pleasure in encouraging them. But you give us no satisfaction. What are your motives in this? Has money in fact lost all appeal for you?"

"I never cared for it," Lafitte said. "You may believe that or not. I cared for justice and freedom. Spain stood against those principles, and so I carried letters of marque to make war upon her. The riches were incidental, necessary merely to prolong that war. But time has moved on. Justice and freedom are antique concepts, of no importance to our modern world. The world, in the person of Lt. Kearny, made it clear that it had no use for me or my kind. I have learned to return the sentiment. I have no use for the things of this world."

He relighted his pipe and took another lungfull of smoke. "You ask about my appearance. I met a brahman from the Indian continent a few years ago. He explained that it is our connection to worldly things that ages us. *Karma,* he called it. I believe I am living proof of the Brahman's beliefs."

"What of those of us still in the world?" Malone said. "I see in you the signs of a former idealist, now disillusioned. I still have ideals. There are still wars to be fought, against ignorance and disease and natural disaster. Wars your treasure could fight. And what of Chighizola, your shipmate? Is he not entitled to his share?" For some reason the fumes from Lafitte's pipe had left Malone terribly hungry. He cast a sideways glance toward the remains of supper.

"If you sailed with him," O'Roarke said to Chighizola, "you must persuade him."

"I think," Chighizola said, "people try that for years now."

"You never answered my question," Malone said to Lafitte. "Money does not motivate you. Neither, it seems, does idealism. At least not any longer. So what is it you care for? What can we offer you?"

"A trip to Galveston," Lafitte said. "I would like to see my island again. To see how things have changed in thirty years. Then we will talk some more." He set his pipe down. "And for the moment, you could hand me the remains of that loaf of bread. I find myself suddenly famished."

THEY OCCUPIED an entire coach on the return trip. Between O'Roarke's spitting and Lafitte's pipe, it was even less pleasant than the outbound journey. They got off the steamer in Galveston late in the evening of a Sunday. The wharf was crowded nonetheless. Several freighters were being filled with cotton, the bales crammed into place with mechanical jackscrews to allow larger loads. The screwmen were the kings of the dock and shouldered their way contemptuously through the newly-arrived passengers, carrying huge bales of cotton on their backs.

Malone led his party, now including a couple of Negro porters, past Water Street to the Strand. It felt good to have the familiar sand and crushed shells under his feet again. "The Tremont Hotel is just over there, on 23rd Street," he said. "If there's any problem with your rooms, just mention the Commercial and Agricultural Bank. Mr. Williams, my employer, is part owner of the hotel."

"And where do *you* live?" Lafitte asked. He had not ceased to smile in the entire time Malone had known him.

"About a mile from here. On 22nd Street. With my wife and her family."

"Do they not have guest rooms?"

"Yes, of course, but it would be awkward…"

"In other words, since this is a purely business venture, you would prefer to put us up like strangers, well away from the sanctity of your home."

"That was never my intent. My wife, you see, is…highly strung. I try not to impose on her, if at all possible."

"We are an imposition, then," Lafitte said. "I see."

"Very well! Enough! You will stop at our house then. We shall manage somehow."

"That is gracious of you," Lafitte said. "I should be delighted."

THERE WAS NO TIME, of course, to warn Becky. Thus Malone arrived on his wife's doorstep with four strangers. He had the porters bring the luggage up the long flight of steps to the porch; like most Galveston houses, it was supported by eight-foot columns of brick.

Jefferson, the Negro butler, answered the door. "Please get the guest room ready," Malone told him. "I shall put a pair of cots in the study as well, I suppose. And tell Mrs. Malone that I have returned."

"Sir."

Chighizola and his woman left with Jefferson. Malone paid the porters and took Lafitte and O'Roarke into the study.

"Nice place," O'Roarke said.

"Thank you," Malone said, painfully pinching a finger as he set up the cots. "Use the cuspidor while in the house, if you do not mind."

Becky appeared in the doorway. "How nice to see you again," she said to Malone, without sincerity. "It would appear your expedition was more successful than you expected."

"This is Mr. O'Roarke and Mr....Lafflin," he said. Lafitte smiled at the name. "This is my wife, Becky."

She sketched a curtsy. "How do you do."

"They are business associates of mine. I regret not letting you know they would be stopping here. It came up rather suddenly."

"I trust you will find a way to explain this to my father. I know it is hopeless to expect you to offer any explanation to me." She turned and disappeared.

"When I lived on the island," Lafitte said, "we had a whorehouse on this very spot."

"Thank you for that bit of history," Malone said. "My night is now complete."

"Is there anything to eat?" O'Roarke asked.

"If you cannot wait until morning, you are welcome to go down to the kitchen and see what you can find. Please do not disturb Jefferson unless you have to." Malone felt sorry for the old Negro. In keeping with current abolitionist sentiment in Texas he had been freed, but his wages consisted of his room and board only. "And now, if you have no objections, I shall withdraw. It is late, and we can resume our business in the morning."

THE HOUSE WAS brutally hot, even with the doors and windows open. There had been a southeast breeze when it was first built; the city's growth had long since diverted it. Malone put on his nightshirt and crawled under the mosquito net. He arranged the big square pillow under his shoulders so that night-borne fevers would not settle in his lungs. Becky lay under the covers, arms pressed against her sides, feigning sleep.

"Good night," he said. She made no answer. He knew that he would be within his rights to pull the covers off and take her, willing or not. She had made it clear she would not resist him. No, she would lie there, eyes closed, soundless, like a corpse. He was almost tempted. The days of confinement with Fabienne had taken their toll.

He could recall the flush of Fabienne's golden skin, her scent, her cascading hair. She would not receive a man so passively, he thought. She could, he imagined, break a man's ribs with the heat of her passion.

Malone got up and drank a small glass of whisky. Imagination had always been his curse. Lately it kept him from sleep and interfered with his accounts. Enough gold, he thought, would cure that. The rich needed no imagination.

MALONE ROSE before his guests, eyes bloodshot and head aching. He scrubbed his face at the basin, dressed, and went downstairs. He found his father-in-law in the breakfast room and quickly put his lies in order. He explained Lafitte and the others as investors, wealthy but eccentric, here to look at the possibility of a railroad causeway to the mainland. Becky's father was mad for progress, in love with the idea of the railroad. He smiled and shook Malone's hand.

"Good work, son," he said. "I knew you would make your mark. Eventually."

Chighizola and Fabienne came down for breakfast at eight. Becky had left word for Cook and there were chafing dishes on the sideboard filled with poached eggs, liver, flounder, sausage, broiled tomatoes, and steak. There was a toast rack, a coffee service, a jug of orange juice, a tray of biscuits, and a large selection of jams in small porcelain pots. O'Roarke joined them shortly before nine. He seemed rather sullen, though he consumed two large plates full of food. He ate in silence, tugging on his orange side whiskers with his left hand.

Lafitte, in contrast, was cheerful when he finally arrived. He was unshaven, without collar, braces, or waistcoat, and his long hair was in disarray. He ate only fish and vegetables and refused Malone's offer of coffee.

When Jefferson came to clear away the dishes Malone asked, "Where is Mrs. Malone this morning?"

"In her room, sir. She said to tell you she had letter writing to see to."

She might come down for supper, then. Unless, of course, she suddenly felt unwell, a condition he could predict with some confidence. "If she asks, you may tell her I have taken our visitors for a walk."

First he showed them St. Mary's cathedral, at 21st Street and Avenue F, with its twin Gothic towers on either side of the arched entranceway. It was barely two years old, the first church on the island and the first cathedral in Texas. To Malone it was a symbol. Virtually the entire city had been rebuilt since 1837 and structures like St. Mary's showed a fresh determination, a resolution to stay no matter what the odds.

He pointed out the purple blossoms of the oleanders that now grew wild all over the city, brought originally from Jamaica in wooden tubs. He led them west to 23rd Street, past Sam Williams' bank. Then he brought them down the Strand, with its commission houses and government offices.

"The similarities to Manhattan Island are clear," Malone said. "Galveston stands as the gateway to Texas, a perfect natural harbor, ideally situated on the Gulf."

"Except for the storms," Lafitte said.

"Man's ingenuity will find a way to rob them of their power. Look around you. This is already the largest city in Texas. And everything you see was brought about by human industry. Nature withheld her hand from this place."

"You need hardly remind me," Lafitte said. "When we first came here there were salt cedars and scrub oaks, poisonous snakes, and man-eating Indians. And nothing else. Am I right, Nez Coupe?"

Chighizola said, "You leave out the malaria and the infernal gulls."

"You can see that things have greatly improved," Malone said.

"Improved? Hardly. I see churches and banks, custom houses and shops, all the fetters and irons of civilization."

"Shops?" O'Roarke said. "Against shops as well, are you? What would you have?"

"No one owned the land when we lived here. Everything was held in common. The prizes we took were divided according to agreed-upon shares. No one went hungry for lack of money."

"Communism," Malone said. "I have heard of it. That German, Karl Marx, has written about it."

"He was hardly the first," Lafitte said. "Bonaparte urged many of the same reforms. As did Rousseau, for that matter."

They had turned east on Water Avenue. At 14th Street Lafitte stopped. He turned back, with one hand shading his eyes, then smiled. "Here," he said.

"Pardon?" Malone asked.

"La Maison Rouge. This is where my house was. Look, you can see where the ground is sunken. This is where I had my moat. Inland stood the gallows. Rebels and mutineers, those who raided any but Spanish ships, died there."

Now there was only an abandoned shack, with wide spaces between the boards where the green wood had shrunk. Malone stepped into its shade for a moment to escape the relentless sun. "Truly?" he said. "Truly, you never attacked an American ship?"

"Truly," Chighizola said. "The Spanish only. He was obsessed."

"Why?"

Chighizola shook his head.

"A private matter," Lafitte said. "I was angry then. Angry enough to burn La Maison Rouge and all the rest of it when I left, burn the entire city to the ground."

"Your anger," Malone said, "is legendary."

"No more," Lafitte said. "To have that much anger, you have to care deeply. To be attached to the world."

"And you care for nothing?" O'Roarke said. "Nothing at all?"

Lafitte shrugged. "Nothing comes to mind."

DINNER WAS LONG and arduous. Lafitte seemed willing enough to play along with Malone's railroad charade. However his lack of seriousness, bordering on contempt, left Becky's father deeply suspicious. O'Roarke's crude speech and spitting would have maddened Becky had she not been upstairs, "feeling poorly," in the words of her maid. As for Chighizola and Fabienne, they were simply ignored.

Afterwards O'Roarke stopped him in the hall. "How much longer? By thunder, Brimstone Jack is not one for waiting around. We should be after the treasure."

"If it is any consolation," Malone said, "I am enjoying this no more than you."

Malone retired, but was unable to sleep. Exhausted, yet with his nerves wound tight, he lay propped up in bed and listened to the clock on the dresser loudly tick away the seconds. He finally reached the verge of sleep, only to come awake again at the sound of someone moving in the hallway.

He dressed hastily and went downstairs. He found Lafitte in the porch glider, smoking his hemp tobacco.

"Might I join you?" Malone asked.

"It is your house."

"No," Malone said, sitting on the porch rail. "It is my wife's house. It is a difference that has plagued me for some time. I crave my independence."

"And you think my treasure will buy that for you."

"That and more. Political power. The ability to change things. To bring real civilization to Galveston, and all of Texas."

"I am no admirer of civilization."

"Yet you fought for this country against the British. You were the hero of New Orleans."

"Yes, I fought for your Union. I was young and foolish, not much older than you. I believed the Union would mean freedom for me and all my men. Instead they pardoned us for crimes we had not committed, then refused to let us make a living. When we removed ourselves to this island of snakes, your Lt. Kearney found us. He came with his laws based on wealth and social position, to tell us we were not to live equally, as brothers. Is this civilization?"

"You cannot judge a country by its frontier. It is always the worst of the old and the new."

"Perhaps. But I have seen New York and Washington, and there the poor are more oppressed than anywhere else. But I shall not convince you of this. You shall have to see it for yourself."

They sat for a few moments in silence. A ship's horn sounded faintly in the distance. "What of your wife?" Lafitte asked. "Do you not love her?"

"Certainly," Malone said. "Why do you ask that?"

"You seem to blame her for your lack of independence."

"Rather she seems to blame me, for my lack of a fortune. It is the same fortune I lacked when she married me."

"She is a lovely woman. I wish there were more happiness between you."

"What of you? Did you ever marry?"

"Once. Long ago."

"Was this in France?"

"I never lived in France. I was born and raised in Santo Domingo. My parents were French." He stopped to relight his pipe. Malone could see him consider whether he would go on or not. At last he said, "They came to the New World to avoid the guillotine. Trouble always found them, just the same. Haiti and Santo Domingo have been fighting since Columbus, two little countries on one island, back and forth, the French against the Spanish, the peasants against the aristocracy."

"And your wife?"

"She was fourteen when we married. I was twenty. She was pledged to a Spanish aristocrat. We eloped. He took her from me by force. She killed herself."

"I—"

Lafitte waved away his apologies. "It was long ago. I took my revenge against Spain, many times over. It proved nothing. I always hoped I would find him on one of the ships we captured. Of course I never did. But as I have said, that was long ago. When my anger, as you say, was legend."

"I do not believe you," Malone said.

Lafitte raised one eyebrow.

"You have told me again and again how you care nothing for things of this world. Yet you nearly destroyed Spanish shipping in the gulf for the sake of a woman, and that pain eats at you still. As does your hatred of Lt. Kearny and everything he stood for. As does your belief in liberty, equality, fraternity. Perhaps I am young, but I have seen men like you, men who numb themselves with alcohol or other substances to convince themselves they have no feelings. My father was one of them. It is not your lack of feeling that has preserved you. It is your passion and committment that has kept you young. Whether you have the courage to admit that or not."

Lafitte sat for at least a minute without moving. Then, slowly, he tapped the ash out of his clay pipe and put it in his coat pocket. He stood up. "Perhaps you are right, perhaps not. But I find myself too weary for argument." He began to descend the stairs to the street.

"Where are you going?"

"Mexico, perhaps. I should thank you for your hospitality."

"What, you mean to simply walk away? With no farewell to Chighizola or the others? All this simply to prove to yourself how unfeeling you are?"

Lafitte shrugged.

"Wait," Malone said. "You are the only hope I have."

"Then you have no hope," Lafitte said, but he paused at the bottom of the steps. Finally he said, "Suppose I took you to the treasure. Tonight. Right now. Would that satisfy you?"

"Are you serious?"

"I do not know. Perhaps."

"Yes, then. Yes, it would satisfy me."

He took another half dozen paces, then turned back. "Well?"

"Am I not to wake the others? To fetch tools? To tell anyone where I am bound?"

"If we are meant to succeed, fate will provide. That is my whim. Come now or lose your chance."

Malone stood, looked uncertainly toward the house. "I will share it with the others," he said. "Just as we agreed. I swear."

"That is your concern, not mine. If you are coming, then come now."

LAFITTE LED HIM to the harbor at a pace too rapid for conversation. The docks still swarmed with activity. With no attempt at stealth Lafitte stepped into a small sailboat. He motioned Malone to silence and gestured for him to get aboard. Malone saw a shovel, a machete, and several gunny sacks on the floor of the boat.

"But…" he said.

Lafitte held a finger to his lips and then pointed it angrily at Malone. Malone untied the stern line and got in. Lafitte rowed them out into the channel. Once they were well away from land Malone whispered, "This is not your boat!"

Lafitte smiled. There was little humor in it. "Do you accuse me of piracy, sir? I warn you I am not fond of the term."

"Is this not theft, at least?"

"Reparations. Owed me by the Republic of Texas and the United States of America. Besides which, you shall have it back before dawn."

Once into Galveston Bay the wind picked up. A chill came off the water and Malone was glad for his coat. In the moonlight the Texas coast was clearly visible, a gray expanse dotted with darker patches of brush. Malone counted at least another dozen sails on the water. Shrimpers, probably, though smuggling was still common. As they passed Jones Point the mainland receded again.

Lafitte was a mediocre sailor at best. He steered them inside South Deer Island, barely avoiding the sandbars. At one point they had to wait for a swell to lift them free. Then, a few minutes later, they rounded a spit of land and headed into Gang's Bayou. It was little better than a swamp, full of marsh grass and sucking mud. Mesquite bushes, with their thorns and spindly branches, grew along the banks around an occasional salt cedar or dwarf willow. It seemed unlikely that Lafitte could hope to find anything in this shifting landscape. Malone began to fear for his life. He should not, he thought, have challenged Lafitte on his lack of feeling.

Lafitte passed one paddle to Malone and kept the other for himself. He lowered the sail and together they pulled the boat into the bayou. The inlet turned quickly around a U-shaped intrusion of land. At the base of it, out of sight of the bay, Lafitte tied up to a squat, massive old oak.

"Bring the shovel," Lafitte said. Malone gathered it up with the gunny sacks. He brought the machete as well, though the thought of violence appalled him. Lafitte took his bearings from the low, marshy ground around them, then drew an X with his boot near the base of the tree. "Dig here," he said.

"How far?"

"Until you strike the chest."

Malone removed his coat and waistcoat and began to dig. He soon lost his chill. Sweat ran into his eyes and his hands began to blister. Lafitte sat a few yards away, uphill on a hummock of grass, smoking his pipe again. The swamp dirt was fine-grained and damp and had a cloying smell of decay. Malone managed a hole three feet around and at least that deep before giving out. It was as if the evil air that came up from the earth had robbed him of his strength.

"I must rest," he said. He laid the shovel by the hole and then crawled over to the trunk of the tree.

"Rest, then," Lafitte said. "I will take a turn."

MALONE FELL into a trance between waking and sleep. He knew he was on Gangs Bayou, on the north shore of Galveston Island. He had lost track of the year. From where he sat it seemed he could see the entire city of Galveston. The streets of the city began to pulse and swell, like an animate creature. Bricks and blocks of quarried stone floated in the air overhead, then alighted on the ground. They formed themselves into towering heaps, not in the shape of houses and churches and schools, but rather in chaotic columns that swayed to impossible heights, blocking the sun. They filled nearly every inch of the island.

Then Malone noticed bits of paper floating in the air between the towers. They seemed to guide the shape of the buildings as they grew. There was printing on the bits of paper and Malone suddenly recognized them. They were paper notes from Sam Williams' C&A Bank. As he watched they folded themselves into halves and quarters and diagonals. He had once seen a Japanese sailor fold paper that way. They made themselves into people and dogs and birds, and they crawled over the crevices between the bricks, as if looking for shelter.

Then, slowly, their edges turned brittle and brown. They began to burn. As they burned the wind carried them toward Malone, who huddled in terror as they began to fall on him.

"Wake up," Lafitte said. "I need your help."

Malone lurched forward, grabbing at nothing. It took him a moment to remember himself. "Forgive me," he said. "I have had the strangest dream. Less a dream than some sort of vision." His head hurt from it, a dull ache that went all the way down his neck.

"Ghosts, most likely," Lafitte said. "They favor treasure. Now come help me get it out of the hole."

"The gold?" Malone said. "You have found it?" It seemed beyond belief.

"See for yourself."

Malone got up and peered into the hole. There did seem to be a sort of trunk there, though mud obscured its details. The top of it was more than four feet down, one end higher than the other. The hole around it, seeping water, was another two feet deep. The thing seemed to have fetched up against the roots of the tree, else it might have sunk to the center of the earth. Malone climbed into the hole and found a handle on one end. Lafitte joined him at the other and together they wrestled the box up onto solid ground.

"Have you the key?" Malone asked, his voice unsteady.

"It is not locked."

Malone used the machete to pry open the lid. Inside he found a greasy bundle of oilcloth. He tugged at it until it unfolded before him.

Even in the moonlight its contents glowed. Gold, silver, precious gems. Malone knelt before it. He took out a golden demitasse and rubbed it against a clean spot on his sleeve. It gleamed like a lantern.

A voice behind him said, "So. This is what you made off to do."

It was O'Roarke. Malone got up to face him. Behind O'Roarke stood Chighizola and the woman. O'Roarke kept walking, right up to Malone. He took the demitasse from Malone's left hand, looked it over, then threw it in the chest. "We thought as long as you were determined to cross us, we would let you do the work. I see now what your promises are worth. You never intended me to gain from all my efforts on your behalf. You merely waited for me to turn my back."

"I swore I would share this with you," Malone stammered, knowing how weak it sounded. "Lafitte witnessed my vow."

"Liar," O'Roarke said. He turned to Lafitte, looming half a foot over him. "And as for you. I should have expected no less from your kind. Once a pirate, always a pirate."

Lafitte slapped him, hard enough to send O'Roarke staggering backward. Malone was suddenly aware of the machete, still in his hand. He wished he were rid of it but was afraid to let it go, afraid to do anything to call attention to himself.

O'Roarke's hand went to his waist. It came up with a pistol, a two-shot derringer. "Die here, then," he said to Lafitte. "Treacherous bastard."

Malone knew he had to act. This was neither dream nor vision, and in a second Lafitte would die. He took a single step forward and swung the machete blindly at O'Roarke's head. O'Roarke's eyes moved to follow the blade and Malone realized, too late, how terribly slow it moved. But O'Roarke turned into the blow and the machete buried itself two inches into his neck.

O'Roarke dropped to his knees. The blade came free, bringing a geyser of blood from the wound. O'Roarke's eyes lost focus and his arms began to jerk. A stain appeared on his trousers and Malone smelled feces, almost indistinguishable from the odor of the swamp. O'Roarke slowly tumbled onto his back, arms and legs quivering like a dreaming dog's.

"Christ," Fabienne said, turning away.

"Finish him, for God's sake," Lafitte said.

Malone was unable to move, unable to look away. He had witnessed violence all his life: the drowned, the mangled, the amputated. But never before had he been the cause.

Chighizola grabbed Malone's arm. "Kill him, you stinking coward, eh? Or I do it myself." The old man jerked the machete from Malone's hand and brought it down swiftly on O'Roarke's neck. It made the same noise as the shovel going into the mud. The head rolled sideways, connected only by a thin strip of skin and muscle, and the hideous tremors stopped.

"So, Lafitte, what you up to here, eh? What tricks you pull now?"

"Whim," Lafitte said. "I thought you did not care for this treasure."

"I do not care to play the fool." He threw the machete toward the hillock and it buried itself in the ground. The man's scars were monstrous, inhuman, in the moonlight. Malone could barely stand to look at them, barely get breath into his lungs. "It makes no difference now," Chighizola said. "The deed is done. Help me put this dead one in the ground."

They dragged O'Roarke's corpse to the hole and threw it in. The head came loose in the process and Chighizola sent it tumbling after the body with a short kick. "So much," he said, "for Brimstone Jack." Malone shoveled mud onto the corpse, eager to see it disappear, to give his shaking hands something to do.

"You have your own boat, I trust," Lafitte said.

Chighizola nodded, then was taken with a bout of coughing. "By Christ, this air is foul. Yes, we...borrowed a felucca from the dock." Chighizola seemed exhausted. Fabienne took him by the arm. When she looked away from him, at either Lafitte or Malone, her face filled with contempt.

"The three of you can take the treasure back in your boat then," Lafitte said. "I shall keep this one for myself."

"You will take none of the gold?" Malone asked.

Lafitte shook his head. "It would only be extra weight."

Fabienne said, "I will help Louis back to the boat. The two of you can manage the trunk."

Malone watched her help Chighizola up the hillock. "This is the end, then. You will simply disappear again into Mexico. To hide in a drunken stupor from a world you have not the courage to change."

Lafitte smiled. "Courage is certainly not something you lack. Not for you to speak to me this way."

"I have come to respect you," Malone said. "I had hoped for better from you."

"Would it please you to know that I have given much thought to your words? All that thought, and now the sight of your gold and the things it has already brought you. Quarrels and deceit and death. For one who is wrong in so many, many ways, you are right in at least one small one. Perhaps it is time to take the lessons of Campeachy to the world. To Europe. Perhaps to this German, Marx. I think we might have much in common."

Malone held out his hand. "I wish you luck."

Lafitte took it. "And I you. I fear you will need it far more than I."

Lafitte got in the boat. "How will you get to Europe without gold?" Malone asked. "What will you have to offer this Marx?"

Lafitte took up the oars, then looked back at Malone. "Life is simpler than you believe it. I hope some day you will see that." He raised one hand and then pushed away from the bank, into darkness.

MALONE DIVIDED the treasure between the two gunny sacks and carried them to the other boat. The sacks must have weighed thirty pounds each. That much gold alone was worth a fortune, even before including the value of the jewels.

Chighizola did not look well. He lay with his head in Fabienne's lap, pale and sweating. Malone rowed them out into the bay, then Fabienne raised the sail. She was far more skillful than Lafitte had been. She took them through the Deer Island sandbars without incident, the water hissing smoothly past the hull.

There was no sign of Lafitte or his boat. He had utterly disappeared.

As the lights of the harbor grew close, Fabienne said, "We shall not return to your house, I think. Louis is very sick. We shall find the first boat headed for New Orleans and be gone this morning."

"I will not argue with you," Malone said. "No more than I would with Lafitte. The agreement was equal shares. You must help me divide it."

She looked at the two sacks. "We will take this one," she said. "You keep the rest."

"As you wish. I shall forward your luggage to you in New Orleans." She had picked, Malone was sure, the smaller of the sacks. His heart filled with joy.

HE TOOK the burlap sack to the carriage house. There he transferred the treasure to a steamer trunk, piece by piece. At the bottom of the sack was a golden thimble. Malone held it up to the lantern. The words CHARITY & HUMILITY were engraved around the inner lip.

He placed the thimble in his waistcoat pocket, locked the trunk, and put it safely away.

He was clean, with his muddy pants and shirt hidden away, by sunrise.

DISCREET INQUIRIES provided Malone with a man in San Felipe willing to dispose of "antiquities" with no questions asked. Malone began to carefully convert the treasure to gold specie, a piece at a time, whenever he travelled north on bank business.

In the fall of 1851 he arranged an invitation to dinner at Sam Williams' house, set on a twenty-acre tract west of the city. Williams was in his mid-fifties now, his hair completely white and parted high on the left side. He was short and heavyset, with a broad forehead and deep lines at the corners of his mouth. He took Malone up to his cupola, where they stood on the narrow walkway and watched for ships in the Gulf. They could hear Williams' daughter Caddy, aged nine, as she played the piano downstairs.

"I understand you have come into some money," Williams said.

"Yes, sir. An inheritance from a long-lost uncle."

"And you are interested in politics."

"Yes, sir."

"There is a good deal an able politician could accomplish these days. I regret I had no knack for it. People found me cold. I do not know why that is." After a moment he said, "You know they are determined to destroy my bank."

"There is a faction, of course, sir, but…"

"Make no mistake, they are out to finish me. They consider me a criminal because I made a profit while I worked for the public good. Why, profit is the heart of this country. It is the very thing that makes us grow. And paper money is essential to that growth. Paper money and venture capitalism. Mark my words. That is where the future lies. You're married to—"

"Becky Kinkaid, sir. John Kinkaid's daughter."

"Yes, a good man. And an important connection. You will want to hold on to her, son, believe me. That name can take you a long way."

"Yes, sir."

"Well, let us see. We can start you out on the city council. It will not be cheap, of course, but then you understand that already."

"Yes, sir."

"Good lad. Nothing like a realistic attitude. You will have need of that."

THERE WAS NEARLY a run on the C&A the following January when a rival bank folded. But Galveston merchants exchanged Robert Mills' paper at par and disaster was narrowly averted. In March the Supreme Court upheld Sam Williams' charter. The anti-bank faction replied with yet another suit, this one based on the illegality of paper money. In April Malone took his seat on the city council and bought his first block of shares in the Commercial and Agricultural Bank.

He found himself with many new friends. They wore tight-fitting suits and brightly colored waistcoats and smoked Cuban cigars. Their opinions became Malone's own by a process he did not entirely understand. But he learned how things were done. A divorce, for example, or even a separation, was not to be considered. Instead he kept a succession of mulatto girls in apartments on the Gulf side of the island, girls with long, curling black hair and unguessable thoughts behind their dark eyes. In time he found that he and Becky could live together with a certain affection and consideration, and it was quite nearly enough. Except for certain hot, muggy nights in the summer when his dreams were haunted by Fabienne.

Still, they were preferable to the nights when he dreamed of towers of stone and folded bank notes and Brimstone Jack O'Roarke with a machete buried in his neck. On those nights he awoke with his hands clutched in the air, on the verge of a scream.

In the next five years he moved from the city council to the Railroad Commission. The next step was the state legislature, via the election in February of 1857. Malone had thought himself a Democrat, but Williams' power lay with the Whigs. The Whigs were traditionally the money party in Texas, and so Malone became a Whig. The campaign was expensive, and took a firm pro-banking stance. On January 19th, banker Robert Mills was fined $100,000 for issuing paper money. Two days later Williams settled out of court on similar

charges, paying a token $2000 fine. Editorials condeming banks and
paper money appeared throughout the state.

The Democrats carried the election. The week after his defeat,
Malone accepted a position on the board of directors of the C&A.

In August the Panic of '57 brought the closure of one bank after
another, all across the country. Tales of bank failures in New Orleans
arrived via steamer on October 16. There was a run on the C&A.
Williams exchanged specie for his own notes, but refused to cash
depositor checks. Malone sat through the night with him, drinking
brandy, waiting to see if the bank would open the next day. They did
open, and Malone brought in the last of the gold coins from his safe
deposit boxes to make sure there would be enough.

That afternoon the bank closed early. Malone stopped for a
whiskey on the way home and found the bartender honoring paper
money at 75 cents on the dollar. Malone saw only fear and resigna-
tion in his eyes. "I got kids, mister," he said. "What can I do? Blame
the bankers."

Williams continued to pay gold the next day. The police came to
keep lines orderly. By noon the fear had gone out of the customers'
eyes. By the end of the month the crisis had passed, only to make
way for a new one: counterfeit C&A notes.

The weeks began to blur. In December, Sam Williams' eldest
son died. In January the Supreme Court postponed another anti-
banking suit, and Williams' lawyers fought delaying actions through
the spring and summer. In the first days of September the yellow
fever came again.

Malone watched the fever take Becky, watched her skin jaundice
and her flesh melt away. Williams' wife Sarah, ever thoughtful, sent
servants with ice to soothe Becky's fever. It was no more use than
Jefferson's herbs. She died on September 7th, a Tuesday.

That Friday Samuel May Williams succumbed to old age and
general debility. He was 62.

It was the end of an era. Malone moved out of Becky's parents'
house and took a suite of rooms on Water Street. The building was
not far from where Lafitte's Maison Rouge had stood. Nothing
remained of the treasure but the golden thimble, which Malone still
carried in the watch pocket of his waistcoat. He sat at his window

and studied the workmen as they built the trestle for the first train from Houston, due to arrive in a little over a year.

He still attended board meetings, though there was little hope the bank could survive. Malone watched with detachment. He saw now how money had a life of its own. For a while he had lived the life of his money, but that life was drawing to a close. The money would go on without him. It was money that had brought the future to Galveston, not Malone. The future would have come without him, in spite of anything he might have done to stop it, had he wanted to. Lafitte had learned that lesson long ago.

He gave up the last of his string of mistresses. The sight of her parents, living on fish heads and stale bread, was more than he could bear. He mounted one final campaign for mayor. His platform advocated better schools, better medicine, a better standard of living. But he was unable to explain where the money would come from. He lost by a landslide.

In March of 1859, the Texas Supreme Court ruled that the Commercial and Agricultural Bank of Texas was illegal. Its doors were closed, its assets liquidated. The last of Malone's money was gone.

HE ARRIVED IN New Orleans early in the morning. The city had grown as much as Galveston had. The changes were even more obvious to his stranger's eye. The old quarter was bordered now by a new business district, with bigger buildings growing up every day.

They still knew Chighizola's name at the market. Many of them had been at his funeral, years before. They knew his children and they remembered the beautiful octoroon with the French name. Malone followed their directions through crowded streets and stopped at an iron gate set into a brick wall. Through the arch he could see a shaded patio, broadleafed plants, small children.

Fabienne answered the bell herself. She was older, her skin a dusty tan instead of gold. Strands of gray showed in her hair. "I know you," she said. "Malone. The hunter of treasure. What do you want here?"

"To give you this," Malone said. He handed her the golden thimble. She took it and turned it over in her hands. "Why?"

"I am not sure. Perhaps as an apology."

She held it out to him. "I do not care for your apology. I do not want anything of yours."

"It is not mine," Malone said. He closed her hand over it and pushed it back toward her. "It never was."

He turned away. A sudden movement in the crowd caught his attention and, for a moment, he thought he looked into the sparkling black eyes of Jean Lafitte, unchanged, despite the years. Malone blinked and the man was gone. It was merely, he thought, another ghost. He took a step, then another, toward the river and the ships. He had enough left for a passage somewhere. He had only to decide where to go.

"Wait," Fabienne said.

Malone paused.

"You have come this far," she said. "The least I can do is offer you a cup of coffee."

"Thank you," Malone said. "I should like a cup of coffee very much."

SECRETS

THEY'D BEEN married sixteen days.

Michael spent a lot of time in the bathroom, as some of her other boyfriends had. So maybe it wasn't entirely an accident when Teresa walked in that night without knocking.

"Sorry," she smiled. "I didn't know—"

Michael was leaning over the lavatory, fully dressed. He had an index finger under each eyelid, pulling it down. A stream of blood poured out of the underside of each eye into the sink.

"Michael?" she whispered.

He turned to look at her. His eyes were rolled back in his head and blood flowed down his cheeks like dark red tears. "GET OUT!" he roared.

In panic she reverted to Spanish: "*Lo siento, lo siento!* I'm sorry!"

When he came to bed it was like nothing had happened. He kissed her forehead and went back to reading his trial transcript. He didn't ask why she shivered at the sight of him.

It was a week before she let him make love to her again. He was so gentle and insistent that she finally gave in. Afterwards, while he slept, she stared at him in the moonlight, searching for strangeness, for some kind of explanation.

She never walked in on him unexpectedly again. As the years went by and she failed to get pregnant she wondered, sometimes, if that was meaningful, if it was related to what she'd seen. The thing that was never mentioned, the thing she tried to tell herself she'd only imagined. The thing she could never forget.

In the end it was Michael who left her. In the ten years they'd been together, he didn't seem to have aged a day. He left her for a younger woman, of course. Theresa thought about calling the woman, trying to warn her, but what could she say?

The feeling eventually passed. Theresa remarried, an older man, a man with few demands or expectations. They had a lovely home, gave many parties, and slept in separate beds.

JEFF BECK

FELIX WAS 34. He worked four ten-hour days a week at Allied Sheet Metal, running an Amada CNC turret punch press. At night he made cassettes with his twin TEAC dbx machines. He'd recorded over a thousand of them so far, over 160 miles of tape, and he'd carefully hand lettered the labels for each one.

He'd taped everything Jeff Beck had ever done, from the Yardbirds' *For Your Love* through all the Jeff Beck Groups and the solo albums; he had the English singles of "Hi Ho Silver Lining" and "Tally Man"; he had all the session work, from Donovan to Stevie Wonder to Tina Turner.

In the shop he wore a Walkman and listened to his tapes. Nothing seemed to cut the sound of tortured metal like the diamond-edged perfection of Beck's guitar. It kept him light on his feet, dancing in place at the machine, and sometimes the sheer beauty of it made tears come up in his eyes.

On Fridays he dropped Karen at her job at *Pipeline Digest* and drove around to thrift shops and used book stores looking for records. After he'd cleaned them up and put them on tape he didn't care about them anymore; he sold them back to collectors and made enough profit to keep himself in blank XLIIs.

Occasionally he would stop at a pawn shop or music store and look at the guitars. Lightning Music on 183 had a Charvel/Jackson soloist, exactly like the one Beck played on *Flash,* except for the hideous lilac-purple finish. Felix yearned to pick it up but was afraid of making a fool out of himself. He had an old Sears Silvertone at home and two or three times a year he took it out and tried to play it, but he could never even manage to get it properly in tune.

Sometimes Felix spent his Friday afternoons in a dingy bar down the street from *Pipeline Digest,* alone in a back booth with a pitcher of Budweiser and an anonymous brown sack of records. On those afternoons Karen would find him in the office parking lot, already asleep in the passenger seat, and she would drive home. She worried a little, but it never happened more than once or twice a month. The rest of the time he hardly drank at all, and he never hit her or chased other women. Whatever it was that ate at him was so deeply buried it seemed easier to leave well enough alone.

ONE THURSDAY afternoon a friend at work took him aside.

"Listen," Manuel said, "are you feeling okay? I mean you seem real down lately."

"I don't know," Felix told him. "I don't know what it is."

"Everything okay with Karen?"

"Yeah, it's fine. Work is okay. I'm happy and everything. I just…I don't know. Feel like something's missing."

Manuel took something out of his pocket. "A guy gave me this. You know I don't do this kind of shit no more, but the guy said it was killer stuff."

It looked like a Contac capsule, complete with the little foil blister pack. But when Felix looked closer the tiny colored spheres inside the gelatin seemed to sparkle in rainbow colors.

"What is it?"

"I don't know. He wouldn't say exactly. When I asked him what it did all he said was, 'Anything you want.'"

HE DROPPED KAREN at work the next morning and drove aimlessly down Lamar for a while. Even though he hadn't hit Half Price Books in a couple of months, his heart wasn't in it. He drove home and got the capsule off the top of his dresser where he'd left it.

Felix hadn't done acid in years, hadn't taken anything other than beer and an occasional joint in longer than he could remember. Maybe it was time for a change.

He swallowed the capsule, put Jeff Beck's *Wired* on the stereo, and switched the speakers into the den. He stretched out on the couch and looked at his watch. It was ten o'clock.

He closed his eyes and thought about what Manuel had said. It would do anything he wanted. So what did he want?

This was a drug for Karen, Felix thought. She talked all the time about what she would do if she could have any one thing in the world. She called it the Magic Wish game, though it wasn't really a game and nobody ever won.

What the guy meant, Felix told himself, was it would make me see anything I wanted to. Like mild hit of psilocybin. A light show and a bit of rush.

But he couldn't get away from the idea. What would he wish for if he could have anything? He had an answer ready; he supposed everybody did. He framed the words very carefully in his mind.

I want to play guitar like Jeff Beck, he thought.

HE SAT UP. He had the feeling that he'd dropped off to sleep and lost a couple of hours, but when he looked at his watch it was only five after ten. The tape was still playing "Come Dancing." His head was clear and he couldn't feel any effects from the drug.

But then he'd only taken it five minutes ago. It wouldn't have had a chance to do anything yet.

He felt different though, sort of sideways, and something was wrong with his hands. They ached and tingled at the same time, and felt like they could crush rocks.

And the music. Somehow he was hearing the notes differently than he'd ever heard them before, hearing them with a certain knowledge of how they'd been made, the way he could look at a piece of sheet metal and see how it had been sheared and ground and polished into shape.

Anything you want, Manuel had said.

His newly powerful hands began to shake.

He went into his studio, a converted storeroom off the den. One wall was lined with tapes; across from it were shelves for the stereo, a few albums, and a window with heavy black drapes. The ceiling and the end walls were covered with gray paper egg cartons, making it nearly soundproof.

He took out the old Silvertone and it felt different in his hands, smaller, lighter, infinitely malleable. He switched off the Beck tape, patched the guitar into the stereo and tried tuning it up.

He couldn't understand why it had been so difficult before. When he hit harmonics he could hear the notes beat against each other with perfect clarity. He kept his left hand on the neck and reached across it with his right to turn the machines, a clean, precise gesture he'd never made before.

For an instant he felt a breathless wonder come over him. The drug had worked, had changed him. He tried to hang on to the strangeness but it slipped away. He was tuning a guitar. It was something he knew how to do.

He played "Freeway Jam," one of Max Middleton's tunes from *Blow By Blow*. Again, for just a few seconds, he felt weightless, ecstatic. Then the guitar brought him back down. He'd never noticed what a pig the Silvertone was, how high the strings sat over the fretboard, how the frets buzzed and the machines slipped. When he couldn't remember the exact notes on the record he tried to jam around them, but the guitar fought him at every step.

It was no good. He had to have a guitar. He could hear the music in his head but there was no way he could wring it out of the Silvertone.

His heart began to hammer and his throat closed up tight. He knew what he needed, what he would have to do to get it. He and Karen had over $1300 in a savings account. It would be enough.

HE WAS HOME again by three o'clock with the purple Jackson soloist and a Fender Princeton amp. The purple finish wasn't nearly as ugly as he remembered it and the guitar fit into his hands like an old lover. He set up in the living room and shut all the windows and played, eyes closed, swaying a little from side to side, bringing his right hand all the way up over his head on the long trills.

Just like Jeff Beck.

He had no idea how long he'd been at it when he heard the phone. He lunged for it, the phone cord bouncing noisily off the strings.

It was Karen. "Is something wrong?" she asked.

"Uh, no," Felix said. "What time is it?"

"Five thirty." She sounded close to tears.

"Oh shit. I'll be right there."

He hid the guitar and amp in his studio. She would understand, he told himself. He just wasn't ready to break it to her quite yet.

In the car she seemed afraid to talk to him, even to ask why he'd been late. Felix could only think about the purple Jackson waiting for him at home.

He sat through a dinner of Chef Boyardee Pizza, using three beers to wash it down, and after he'd done the dishes he shut himself in his studio.

For four hours he played everything that came into his head, from blues to free jazz to "Over Under Sideways Down" to things he'd never heard before, things so alien and illogical that he couldn't translate the sounds he heard. When he finally stopped Karen had gone to bed. He undressed and crawled in beside her, his brain reeling.

HE WOKE UP to the sound of the vacuum cleaner. He remembered everything, but in the bright morning light it all seemed like a weirdly vivid hallucination, especially the part where he'd emptied the savings account.

Saturday was his morning for yard work, but first he had to deal with the drug business, to prove to himself that he'd only imagined it. He went into the studio and lifted the lid of the guitar case and then sat down across from it in his battered blue-green lounge chair.

As he stared at it he felt his love and terror of the guitar swell in his chest like cancer.

He picked it up and played the solo from "Got the Feelin'" and then looked up. Karen was standing in the open door.

"Oh my god," she said. "Oh my god. What have you done?"

Felix hugged the guitar to his chest. He couldn't think of anything to say to her.

"How long have you had this? Oh. You bought it yesterday, didn't you? That's why you couldn't even remember to pick me up." She slumped against the door frame. "I don't believe it. I don't *even* believe it."

Felix looked at the floor.

"The bedroom air conditioner is broken," Karen said. Her voice sounded like she was squeezing it with both hands; if she let it go it would turn into hysteria. "The car's running on four bald tires. The TV looks like shit. I can't remember the last time we went out to dinner or a movie." She pushed both hands into the sides of her face, twisting it into a mask of anguish.

"How much did it cost?" When Felix didn't answer she said, "It cost everything, didn't it? *Everything.* Oh god, I just can't believe it."

She closed the door on him and he started playing again, frantic scraps and tatters, a few bars from "Situation," a chorus of "You Shook Me," anything to drown out the memory of Karen's voice.

It took him an hour to wind down, and at the end of it he had nothing left to play. He put the guitar down and got in the car and drove around to the music stores.

On the bulletin board at Ray Hennig's he found an ad for a guitarist and called the number from a pay phone in the strip center outside. He talked to somebody named Sid and set up an audition for the next afternoon.

When he got home Karen was waiting in the living room. "You want anything from Safeway?" she asked. Felix shook his head and she walked out. He heard the car door slam and the engine shriek to life.

He spent the rest of the afternoon in the studio with the door shut, just looking at the guitar. He didn't need to practice; his hands already knew what to do.

The guitar was almost unearthly in its beauty and perfection. It was the single most expensive thing he'd ever bought for his own pleasure, but he couldn't look at it without being twisted up inside by guilt. And yet at the same time he lusted for it passionately, wanted to run his hands endlessly over the hard, slick finish, bury his head in the plush case and inhale the musky aroma of guitar polish, feel the strings pulse under the tips of his fingers.

Looking back he couldn't see anything he could have done differently. Why wasn't he happy?

When he came out the living room was dark. He could see a strip of light under the bedroom door, hear the snarling hiss of the TV. He felt like he was watching it all from the deck of a passing ship; he could stretch out his arms but it would still drift out of his reach.

He realized he hadn't eaten since breakfast. He made himself a sandwich and drank an iced tea glass full of whiskey and fell asleep on the couch.

A LITTLE after noon on Sunday he staggered into the bathroom. His back ached and his fingers throbbed and his mouth tasted like a kitchen drain. He showered and brushed his teeth and put on a clean T-shirt and jeans. Through the bedroom window he could see Karen lying out on the lawn chair with the Sunday paper. The pages were pulled so tight that her fingers made ridges across them. She was trying not to look back at the house.

He made some toast and instant coffee and went to browse through his tapes. He felt like he ought to try to learn some songs, but nothing seemed worth the trouble. Finally he played a Mozart symphony that he'd taped for Karen, jealous of the sound of the orchestra, wanting to be able to make it with his hands.

The band practiced in a run-down neighborhood off Rundberg and IH35. All the houses had large dogs behind chain link fences and plastic Big Wheels in the driveways. Sid met him at the door and took him back to a garage hung with army blankets and littered with empty beer cans.

Sid was tall and thin and wore a black Def Leppard T-shirt. He had acne and blond hair in a shag to his shoulders. The drummer and bass player had already set up; none of them looked older than 22 or 23. Felix wanted to leave but he had no place else to go.

"Want a brew?" Sid asked, and Felix nodded. He took the Jackson out of its case and Sid, coming back with the beer, stopped in his tracks. "Wow," he said. "Is that your ax?" Felix nodded again. "Righteous," Sid said.

"You know any Van Halen?" the drummer asked. Felix couldn't see anything but a zebra striped headband and a patch of black hair behind the two bass drums and the double row of toms.

"Sure," Felix lied. "Just run over the chords for me, it's been a while." Sid walked him through the progression for "Dance the

Night Away" on his 3/4 sized Melody Maker and the drummer counted it off. Sid and the bass player both had Marshall amps and Felix's little Princeton, even on ten, got lost in the wash of noise.

In less than a minute Felix got tired of the droning power chords and started toying with them, adding a ninth, playing a modal run against them. Finally Sid stopped and said, "No, man, it's like this," and patiently went through the chords again, A, B, E, with a C# minor on the chorus.

"Yeah, okay," Felix said and drank some more beer.

They played "Beer Drinkers and Hell Raisers" by ZZ Top and "Rock and Roll" by Led Zeppelin. Felix tried to stay interested, but every time he played something different from the record Sid would stop and correct him.

"Man, you're a hell of a guitar player, but I can't believe you're as good as you are and you don't know any of these solos."

"You guys do any Jeff Beck?" Felix asked.

Sid looked at the others. "I guess we could do 'Shapes of Things,' right? Like on that Gary Moore album?"

"I can fake it, I guess," the drummer said.

"And could you maybe turn down a little?" Felix said.

"Uh, yeah, sure," Sid said, and adjusted the knob on his guitar a quarter turn.

Felix leaned into the opening chords, pounding the Jackson, thinking about nothing but the music, putting a depth of rage and frustration into it he never knew he had. But he couldn't sustain it; the drummer was pounding out 2 and 4, oblivious to what Felix was playing, and Sid had cranked up again and was whaling away on his Gibson with the flat of his hand.

Felix jerked his strap loose and set the guitar back in its case.

"What's the matter?" Sid asked, the band grinding to a halt behind him.

"I just haven't got it today," Felix said. He wanted to break that pissant little toy Gibson across Sid's nose, and the strength of his hatred scared him. "I'm sorry," he said, clenching his teeth. "Maybe some other time."

"Sure," Sid said. "Listen, you're really good, but you need to learn some solos, you know?"

Felix burned rubber as he pulled away, skidding through a U-turn at the end of the street. He couldn't slow down. The car fishtailed when he rocketed out onto Rundberg and he nearly went into a light pole. Pounding the wheel with his fists, hot tears running down his face, he pushed the accelerator to the floor.

KAREN WAS GONE when Felix got home. He found a note on the refrigerator: "Sherry picked me up. Will call in a couple of days. Have a lot to think about. K."

He set up the Princeton and tried to play what he was feeling and it came out bullshit, a jerkoff reflex blues progression that didn't mean a thing. He leaned the guitar against the wall and went into his studio, shoving one tape after another into the decks, and every one of them sounded the same, another tired, simpleminded rehash of the obvious.

"I didn't ask for this!" he shouted at the empty house. "You hear me? This isn't what I asked for!"

But it was, and as soon as the words were out he knew he was lying to himself. Faster hands and a better ear weren't enough to make him play like Beck. He had to change inside to play that way, and he wasn't strong enough to handle it, to have every piece of music he'd ever loved turn sour, to need perfection so badly that it was easier to give it up than learn to live with the flaws.

He sat on the couch for a long time and then, finally, he picked up the guitar again. He found a clean rag and polished the body and neck and wiped each individual string. Then, when he had wiped all his fingerprints away, he put it back into the case, still holding it with the rag. He closed the latches and set it next to the amp, by the front door.

For the first time in two days he felt like he could breathe again. He turned out all the lights and opened the windows and sat down on the couch with his eyes closed. Gradually his hands became still and he could hear, very faintly, the fading music of the traffic and the crickets and the wind.

THE BEST PART
OF MAKING UP

"SEE?" Michael said. "You did, in fact, tell me to go to hell." He played the tape again.

"Yeah, but you were the one that was shouting." Marianne folded her arms across her chest.

"I was not."

Marianne punched up peak level displays and froze the next section of tape. "See? Into the red."

Michael sighed. "I'm tired of fighting. Can't we watch that time we made love at the beach?"

DIRTY WORK

For Joe R. Lansdale

THE OFFICE smelled like money. Brand new carpet, somebody's expensive perfume still hanging in the air. The chairs in the waiting room are leather and the copy machine has a million attachments and there's pictures on the wall that I don't know what they're supposed to be. Made me ashamed of the shirt I was wearing, the cuffs all frayed and some of the buttons don't match.

The secretary is a knockout and I figure Dennis has got to be getting in her pants. Red hair and freckles and shiny skin that looks like she just got out of a hot shower. A smile like she really means it. My name was in the book and she showed me right on in.

Dennis shook my hand and put me in a chair that was slings and tube steel. The calendar next to his desk had a ski scene on it. Behind him was solid books, law books all in the same binding, also some biographies and political stuff.

"Too bad you couldn't make the reunion," Dennis said. "It was a hoot."

"I just felt weird about it," I said. I still did. It looked like he wanted me to go on, so I said, "I knew there'd be a bunch of y'all there that had really made good, and I guess I…I don't know. Didn't want to have to make excuses."

"Hard to believe it's been twenty years. You look good. I still wouldn't want to run into you in a dark alley, but you look fit. In shape."

"I got weights in the garage, I try to work out. When you're my size you can go to hell pretty quick. You look like you're doing pretty good yourself." Charlene is always pointing to people on TV and talking about the way they dress. With Dennis I could see for the first time what she's talking about. The gray suit he had on looked like part of him, like it was alive. When I think about him in grungy sweats back at Thomas Jefferson High School, bent double from trying to run laps, it doesn't seem like the same guy.

"Can't complain," Dennis said.

"Is that your Mercedes downstairs? What do they call those, SLs?"

"My pride and joy. Can't afford it, of course, but that's what bankers are for, right? You were what, doing something in oil?"

"Rig foreman. You know what that means. 'I'm not saying business is bad, but they're telling jokes about it in Ethiopia.'"

Dennis showed me this smile that's all teeth and no eyes. "Like I told you on the phone. I can't offer you much. The technical name for what you'll be is a paralegal. Usually that means research and that kind of thing, but in your case it'll be legwork."

Beggars can't be choosers. What Dennis pays for his haircut would feed Charlene and the kids for close to a week. I must look ten years older than him. All those years in the sun put the lines in your face and the ache in your bones. He was eighteen when we graduated, I was only seventeen, now I'm the one that's middle aged. He was tennis, I was football. Even in high school he was putting it to girls that looked like that secretary of his. Whereas me and Charlene went steady from sophomore year, got married two weeks after graduation. I guess I've been to a couple of topless bars, but I've never been with anybody else, not that way.

It was hard for me to call Dennis up. What it was, I got the invitation for the class reunion, and they had addresses for other people in the class. Seemed like fate or something, him being right here in Austin and doing so good. I knew he'd remember me. Junior year a couple of guys on the team were waiting for him in the parking lot to hand him his ass, and I talked them out of it. That was over a girl too, now that I think about it.

Dennis said, "I got a case right now I could use some help with." He slid a file over from the corner of the desk and opened it up. "It's a rape case. You don't have a problem with that, do you?"

"What do you mean?"

Dennis sat back, kind of studying me, playing with the gold band on his watch. "I mean my client is the defendant. The thing is—and I'm not saying it's this way all the time or anything—but a lot of these cases aren't what you'd think. You got an underage girl, or married maybe, gets caught with the wrong jockey in her saddle, she hollers 'rape' and some guy goes to the slammer for nothing. Nothing you and I haven't ever done, anyway."

"So is this one of those cases?"

"It's a little fishy. The girl is at UT, blonde, good family, the guy is the wrong color for Mom and Dad. Maybe she wanted a little rough fun and then got cold feet. The point is, the guy gets a fair trial, no matter what he did." He took a form out of the file. "I'll get you a xerox of this. All I want is for you to follow this broad around for a couple of days, just kind of check her out."

"How do you mean?"

"Just get an idea of what kind of person she is. Is she some little ice princess, like she wants the DA to believe? Or is she showing her panties to anybody with a wallet and a dick?"

"Geez, Dennis, I really don't know…"

"There's nothing to it. This is absolutely standard procedure in a case like this. She knows she's going to have people watching her, it's just part of the legal bullshit game." When I didn't say anything he said, "It's ten bucks an hour, time-and-a-half if you go over forty hours a week, which I don't see this doing. We pay you cash, you're responsible for your own taxes and like that, and if you forget to declare it, that's your lookout. Hint hint. If this works out we can probably find some other things for you."

Here's the carrot, was what he was saying, and here's the stick. Good money, tax free, if you do it. Turn this case down because it sounds a little hinky and you're back on the street.

"What's this woman's name?"

"Some horrible yuppie name…" He looked at the file. "Lane, that's it. Lane Rochelle. Isn't that a hoot?"

I didn't like the way her name made me feel. Like I was standing outside the window of one of those big Highland Park mansions back in Dallas, wearing last week's clothes, watching guys in tuxedos and women in strapless dresses eat little sandwiches with the crusts cut off. I blamed her for it. "I don't know anything about this kind of work," I said. "I mean, if she sees me I'm liable to scare her off. I don't exactly blend into a crowd."

"Let her see you. It's not a problem."

I still wasn't sure. "When would you want me to start?"

He slapped me on the shoulder as he came around the desk. "There you go," he said. He walked out of the office and I heard the hum of his big new copy machine.

So I DROVE OVER to campus in my good corduroy jacket and my frayed cuffs and my black knit tie. I parked my pickup in the Dobie garage and walked down 21st Street to the Perry Casteneda Library, where Lane Rochelle works. The piece of paper Dennis gave me shows her address and her job history and her criminal record (NONE). Also a xerox of a photo of her from the society page of the *Statesman*.

She's older than Dennis let on, twenty-eight, she's working on her master's degree in History. She's paying her own way with her job at the library, not living off her rich parents back in Virginia, which makes me like her more too. The photo doesn't tell me much. Blonde hair, nice smile, wears her clothes the way Dennis wears his.

I went past the security guard and the turnstiles and looked around. I mean, I don't spend a lot of time in libraries. The place is big and there's this smell of old paper that makes me a little sick to my stomach. The Circulation desk is off to my left and across from it there are some shelves with new books and a yellow naugahyde couch. I found a book that looked interesting, a true-crime thing about this guy that kept a woman in a box. I sat down and every so often looked up and finally I caught sight of Lane moving around behind the counter.

She's not an ice princess, and she's not some kind of sexpot either. She's just a real person, maybe a little prettier than most. Right then she looked like somebody that didn't get a lot of sleep the night before and is having a tough day. The second time she caught me looking at her I saw it hit home—some big guy lurking around her job. I hated to see the look on her face, which was mostly fear.

A little before eleven o'clock she came out a door to one side of the counter with her purse and a bookbag. I let her get out the front door and then followed. It was nice out, warmer than you could ask February to be. The trees had their first buds, which would all die if it froze again. There were even birds and everything. She headed up 21st Street and turned at the Littlefield fountain, the one with the horses, and climbed the steps toward the two rows of buildings on top of the hill. Once she looked back and I turned away, crouched down to pretend to tie my shoe, not fooling anybody.

I watched her go in the first building on the left, the one with the word MUSIC over the door. I followed her inside. The halls were full of students and I watched her push through them and go in one of the classrooms. Just before she went in she turned and gave me this look of pure hatred.

Made me feel pretty low. I stood there for ten minutes just the same, after the hall cleared and the bell rang, to make sure she stayed put. Then I went outside and walked around the side of the building. The classrooms all had full-length windows. The top halves were opened out to let in the warm air. I found Lane's room and sat in the grass, watching a woman teacher write on the board. She had heavy legs and glasses and dark hair in a pony tail. Charlene always talks about going back to college, but I can't see it, not for me. I had a semester of junior college, working construction all day and sleeping through class at night. They didn't have football scholarships and I wasn't good enough for the four-year colleges that did. So I went with what I knew and took a a job on my daddy's drilling crew.

By eleven thirty I was starving to death. There was a Vietnamese woman with a pushcart down by the fountain selling eggrolls. I walked down there and got me a couple and a Coke and took them back up the hill to eat. It would have been okay, really, eating eggrolls outside on a pretty spring day and getting paid for it. Only Lane knew I was there watching and I could see what it was doing to her.

At noon we went back to the library. Lane sat off to herself in the shelves behind the counter. She had brought her lunch in her bookbag, a carton of yogurt and a Diet Coke. She didn't seem to be able to eat much. After a couple of bites she threw it away and went to the rest room.

She got off work at two in the afternoon. I watched her climb on a shuttlebus and then I drove out to her apartment and waited for her. She has a one-bedroom on 53rd street near Airport, what they call a mixed neighborhood—black, white, brown, all low-income. This is where the rape happened. There's a swimming pool that doesn't look too clean and a couple of 70s muscle cars up on blocks. A lot like my neighborhood, over on the far side of Manor Road.

She walked right past me on her way to her apartment. I was sitting in my truck, watching the shuttlebus pull away. She went right past me. I could tell by the set of her shoulders that she knew I was there. She went in her apartment, toward the near end of the second floor, and I could hear the locks click shut from where I sat. She pulled the blinds and that was it.

I did what Dennis told me. I got out and made a log of all the cars parked along the street there, make and model and license number, and then I went on home.

I WAS IN TIME to give the kids a ride back from the bus stop. Ricky is fifteen and going through this phase where he doesn't talk except to say yes or no to direct questions. Mostly he shrugs and shakes his head in amazement at how stupid adults are. So naturally he didn't say anything about me wearing a tie. Judy, who is seventeen, wouldn't let it alone. "What's it for, Dad? You look way cool. You messing around? Got a girlfriend?" She doesn't mean anything by it, she's just kidding.

I had TV dinners in the oven by the time Charlene got home. Salisbury steak, mashed potatoes, and that apple cobbler desert she loves. Her new issue of *Vogue* was there and she took it into the bathroom with her for a while. When she came out she was showered and in her blue-gray bathrobe and fuzzy slippers, with her hair in a towel. She loves *Vogue* magazine. I guess it takes her to some other world, where she isn't pushing forty and she still weighs what she did in high school and she doesn't spend all her days answering phones for a heating and air conditioning company.

"How'd it go?" she said. We had *Wheel of Fortune* on, the kids on the floor with their dinners between us and the TV.

"I got four hours in today, ten bucks an hour. I should make at least that tomorrow."

"That wasn't what I asked."

One reason I never ran around on Charlene is I don't think I could fool her for a second. "I don't like it," I said. "I think he's using me to scare somebody, because I'm big and ugly."

Charlene grabbed the back of my neck and shook me like a cat. "You're big all right. But I always thought you was handsome." Then she leaned back and picked up her magazine again and she was gone.

EVERYBODY WAS asleep by eleven. I went out real quiet and drove over to Lane's apartment. There were a lot more cars out front this time and I wrote down all the new ones on my log sheet. The light was still on in her apartment. I was about to head home when the blinds moved and she looked out and saw my truck.

I wanted out of there bad enough that I made the tires on that pickup squeal.

I SLEPT AWHILE and then laid awake awhile and then it was morning. I had a lot of coffee and not too much to eat which made my stomach hurt.

I was already at the library when Lane came in. She saw me and went straight through the STAFF door and stayed out of sight. A few minutes later a campus cop knocked on the door and she stood in the doorway with him and pointed me out.

I felt like high school again, like I'd been caught with a *Playboy* in the toilet. The campus cop walked walked over and asked me if I had any ID. I showed him my driver's license.

"What you up to here?"

I gave him one of Dennis's cards, like Dennis said I should. "I'm doing research for a law office. Call this number, they'll back me up."

"Don't look like you're doing research to me. Maybe you should move along."

"Fine," I said. I put my book back on the shelf, which was too bad because it had gotten interesting. Only I couldn't check it out because I wasn't a student. I went outside and sat on a wall.

It was a nice day for something. Warm again, a few clouds, the birds getting ready for spring. College girls all around. I never saw so many good-looking girls in one place. Young and healthy, in tight jeans and running shoes, clean soft hair blowing around, sweet smells trailing along behind them. It hurts to see so much that you want, that you can never have, to be so close you could reach out and touch it.

About a half hour later Lane came out of the library and headed down Speedway, right through the middle of campus. I didn't think she saw me. I found myself noticing the way she walked, the way her young, firm ass strained against her jeans. Don't even think about it. I waited until she had a good lead on me before I started after her.

She turned left on 24th Street, by the Experimental Science building, and I lost sight of her. When I turned the corner she was gone. I hesitated for a second, kids shouldering by me on both sides and then I went up to the first door I came to and looked inside. Not there.

When I turned around she was right in front of me. "What do you want?" she said. She was shaking and her voice was too loud.

"I'm working for a lawyer—"

"That defense lawyer? That fuck? Did he hire you to follow me around? What the fuck does he want from me? Is this Gestapo bull-shit supposed to make me drop the case?"

"I don't think he—"

"What kind of slimebag are you, anyhow? Haven't I had enough shit already? How can you stand to go around and humiliate people this way?" Crying now, people stopping to stare at us. "Do you know what happened this morning? My boss called me in and wanted to know why I was being followed. Like it was my fault! I had to tell him everything. Everything! Can you imagine how humiliating that was? No. Of course you can't. If you could imagine it you would go shoot yourself."

A boy walked up and put his hand on her arm. She shook it off and shouted at him, too. "Leave me the fuck *alone!*" She turned back to me, her mascara running all over her face, and spit on my left shoe. Then she shoved her way through the crowd and started running back down Speedway, back the way she came.

I STARTED SHAKING too, as soon as I got in the truck. I shook all the way to Dennis' office.

He was with "one of his people" when I came in. After a few minutes his door opened and this good-looking Chicano came out. He was in his twenties, with longish hair and a mustache and an expensive black leather coat that hung down to his knees. He smiled at the red haired receptionist and pointed at her and said, "You be good, now."

"You too, Javier."

"No chance," he said, and rubbed his mustache and sniffed. The receptionist laughed. I couldn't help but think that Dennis was paying him more than ten bucks an hour for whatever it was he did.

Dennis was standing in the doorway of his office. "Come on in," he said.

I sat on the edge of the armchair. It wasn't really built for that and it made me feel off-balance. There was a dusty-looking mirror and a soda straw on his desk.

"You want a little toot?"

I shook my head. "It's about this case. This is really nasty. I don't know if I can go on with it."

"Okay," he said. He put the mirror and the straw in the top center drawer and then got a bank bag out of another one. It was one of those rubberized deals with the zipper and the little lock, except it wasn't zipped or locked. "How many hours did you have?"

I guess I expected him to argue with me at least, maybe even offer me something else. "Call it seven," I said. "And two parking receipts." I put my log sheet with the license numbers on it and the receipts on the corner of his desk. I felt small sitting there, just waiting for him to pay me.

"So what happened?" he said.

"She turned on me, started screaming. Said I was trying to scare her off."

"Gave you the old not-a-moment's-peace bit, right?" He counted out four twenties and put them in front of me. "Haven't got any singles, you can keep the change."

"Something like that, yeah."

"Well, I understand. If you can't hack it…"

"It's not that I can't hack it, I just don't see why I should want to."

Dennis sat back in his chair. Today he was wearing his casual outfit. I'd never seen a silk jacket before, but Charlene had showed me pictures and I was pretty sure that's what it was. The pants were khaki, the shirt was pale blue, the shoes had little tassels on them. "Let me explain something to you. This business isn't about who makes the most noise or who sheds the most tears. At least it's not supposed to be. It's about the *truth*. And the truth is not always what it seems. Ever have some asshole nearly run you off the road, and then he gives *you* the finger? A guilty conscience can make for a lot of righteous-sounding anger. This Rochelle bimbo has been going to one of those dyke counselling centers, and who knows what kind of crap they've been feeding her."

"But what if she's telling the truth?"

"If she is, my client goes to jail, probably does ten years of hard time. If she's lying, she could go up herself for perjury. These are not matchsticks we're playing for, here." He leaned forward again. Every time he moved he did something different with his voice and I felt my emotions getting yanked around in another direction. "Look, I understand where you're coming from. It takes a while to build up your callouses. Just like working on an oil rig, right? You get a lot of blisters at first and it hurts like hell. Then you toughen up and you can really get the job done." He put the bank bag in the drawer. "Take the afternoon off, think it over. If you still want out, call me tonight, I'll put somebody else on the case. I'll be here in the office, I'm working late all week. Okay?"

"Okay," I said. I took the small stack of bills and folded it and put it in my front pants pocket. I wondered when was the last time Dennis got a blister on his hands.

As I got up he said, "Just one thing you want to keep in mind. Everybody's got something to hide."

I CAN'T REMEMBER the last time I had that much cash in my pocket. It made me a little drunk. I drove to the Victoria's Secret store at Highland Mall and spent $58 on a crepe de chine sarong-wrap chemise in mango, size L. I took it home and hid it in the bedroom, and all through supper I was goofy as a little kid, just thinking about it.

I gave it to Charlene after we went to bed. She started crying. She said, "I'll get back on my diet tomorrow. It's so beautiful. I can't wear it the way I look now." She put it in the back of her drawer. She didn't even try it on.

She kissed me on the cheek and lay down with her back to me. I sat there, my hands all knotted up into fists. After a while she went to sleep.

I just sat there. I hadn't called Dennis. I was supposed to call him if I wasn't going back on the job. If I didn't do it he would just get somebody else. Somebody with all those callouses I don't have. Finally I got up and put my clothes back on and went out driving.

I guess I was supposed to be thinking things over, but what I did was drive to Lane Rochelle's apartment. It was a quarter to twelve. I wrote the time down on a new log sheet and walked around and wrote down all the cars and license numbers. Lane's window was dark. I got back in the truck and tried to find a comfortable way to sit. I wondered what she wore to bed. Maybe it was a crepe de chine sarong-wrap chemise in mango, size S. Maybe it was nothing at all.

A car door slammed and woke me up. The digital clock on my dash said one AM. I saw a guy walking away from a black Trans Am, two slots down on the right. It was the guy I saw in Dennis' office that afternoon. I slid a little lower in the seat.

I wondered what was he doing there? Did Dennis give him my job? He went through the gate by the pool, headed for the far set of stairs.

The apartments are kind of L-shaped, with the long part parallel to the street and the short part coming toward where I was. There was another set of stairs on the end of the building closest to me. I got out of the truck as quiet as I could and went up the stairs. I got to the corner just as the guy knocked on Lane's door.

I could hear my heart. It sounded like it was in my neck. The guy knocked again, louder this time. I heard the door open and catch on its chain.

"Javier," Lane said. She sounded only a little surprised.

"I got your message," the guy, Javier, said.

"It's late. What time is it?"

"Not that late. You gonna let me in or what?"

"Not tonight. Come back tomorrow, okay?"

"Listen, I went to a lot of trouble to drive over here. How about a beer or something, anyway?"

"Fuck off." I wondered where she learned to talk like that. "Come back tomorrow night."

The door slammed and two or three locks turned. I didn't hear any footsteps. Javier was still standing there. Then he said, "*Chingase, puta!*" and walked away.

I moved away from the corner and pushed my back flat against the wall. I was in the shadows, I didn't think he could see me. He took one last look at Lane's apartment and then spit in the swimming pool and got in his Trans Am and drove away.

I WAS COVERED in sweat when I got home. I had to sponge myself off with a wet washcloth before I could get back into bed. Charlene was still asleep, snoring away.

I wondered if I should call Dennis. What if he already knew Javier was hanging around? What if it was his idea? I thought about the smooth way he handled me that afternoon in his office and decided it wasn't any of my business. If Dennis wanted to ask me a question I would answer it. Otherwise I was on my own.

Being on my own is okay. I've been that way most of my life. It makes some things a lot easier. Like taking Dennis' money.

I GOT TO the library about ten o'clock and went right up to the circulation desk. Lane was there and when she saw me she turned and walked away. This older woman came over and asked if she could help me.

"I need to talk to Lane for a second."

"What is this in reference to?"

"It's in reference to I would like to apologize to her."

The old lady went to talk to Lane. They went back and forth a little and at one point the old lady put her arms around Lane and gave her a hug. It made me feel lonely to look at them like that. Then Lane came up to the counter. She took hold of the edge with both hands and waited for me to talk.

"Look," I said. "I'm sorry I scared you. I've been out of work for two years. This is just a job to me." She stared, no expression. "I thought about the things you said, and maybe I don't trust this lawyer very much either. What I'm trying to say is, you don't have anything to be afraid of from me. If you're…I mean, if things are the way you say they are, I would maybe like to help a little if I could."

She stared a while longer, and then she said, very quiet, "If you want to help, just go away. Just get the fuck away from me and stay out of my life."

"I can't do that right now," I said. "I have this job to do and it's the only thing I've got. All I want is to try to make the best of it."

Her eyes teared up. "Make the best of it. Oh God. What do you know about anything?"

She walked away and there was no use calling her back. I got my true crime book again and took it over by the card catalog, where I could see her if she left the building but she wouldn't have to watch me hang around all day. At eleven I followed her to her class at the Music building and back again after. I had an eggroll lunch while I waited and if she noticed me she didn't let on.

It was another nice day. I sat outside until she left at two, watching the clouds move around in the sky. She got on her shuttlebus and I sat there a little longer, wishing things were different but not knowing what exactly I would change. Just a mood, I guess. Then I started the long uphill walk back to the Dobie Garage.

Dobie is the only place a non-student can park anywhere near the library. It's across from Dobie Mall, which is this combination shopping center and dormitory. Kids can eat, shop, sleep, go to movies, have sex, live and die there without ever going outside. The garage is always full so I had to park on the fourth level, one down from the roof. Homeless guys, what we used to call winos, what the kids call Drag worms, sleep in the stairwells, which smell of them peeing and throwing up there. I can't stand to see those guys, I want to knock them down to get away from them. If it wasn't for Charlene that could be me. No work, no future.

I got up to level four and even from the end of the row I could tell something was wrong. The truck was not sitting right. I felt sick. It goes back to my days on the rigs. Your wheels are your livelihood.

If you can't get around, you can't work, if you can't work you can't feed yourself, if you can't do that you're not a man anymore.

I wanted to run over and see what was wrong and at the same time I wanted it not to be happening and the two things were pulling me in opposite directions. By the time I got to the truck my heart was pounding and my eyes were blurry.

It was all four tires flat. They weren't cut, not that I could see. The valve stem covers were off and they'd let the air out with a Bic pen or something. In addition they had taken their car keys or something and put long, ugly scratches down both sides of the body. I walked all the way around and then I started kicking one of the tires, which was stupid. It wasn't the tire that had done it.

It wasn't Lane that had done it either. She wasn't out of my sight all morning.

There was a note under the windshield wiper. It was in block capitals on lined yellow legal paper. It said GO AWAY.

I CALLED the Triple A and they sent a truck. The driver said something about those fucking college kids and I nodded along. While he was doing the tires I looked under the frame and inside the hood to make sure there wasn't a bomb or anything. Then I had the guy wait to make sure it started, which it did.

I stopped off at Airport Auto Supply and got some white primer and sprayed it on the scratches and it didn't look quite so bad. Then I went home. I wasn't shaking this time, not outside. It was all inside. It's like the constant vibration from the rotary table out on the drilling platform. It goes right through you. The kids were already there so I went out in the back yard and looked at the dead yellow grass. There were patches of green coming through and every one was a weed.

Call Dennis. He can get the note fingerprinted.

Sure. Students use legal pads, but so do lawyers. Maybe it was his cocaine buddy Javier did my tires. I can handle him one on one, but I know he's the kind of guy carries a gun.

The house needs a paint job, the lawn needs a gardener. The kids are nearly old enough for college and I got no money to send them.

I wish I had a Mercedes SL instead of a Pinto wagon and a Ford pickup truck. I need a drink but I don't dare start. When was the last time I thought about who I am, instead of what I have? When did it start being the same thing?

In the bedroom, on the bottom of my undershirt drawer, was my daddy's gun. A Colt Woodsman .22 target pistol, loaded, because my daddy taught me an unloaded gun is worse than no gun at all. I went in the bedroom and locked the door and got it out. It smelled of oil and a little bit like cedar from the drawer. It felt great in my hand. I made sure the safety was on and stuck it in my pants. No, that was stupid. It would fall out or I would shoot myself in the foot. I folded it up in an old Dallas Cowboys nylon jacket.

Charlene was home. I heard her try the bedroom door, then knock quietly. I opened it. "I need to use the wagon," I said.

We never ask each other a lot of questions. It's like we don't really know how to go about it. I could see her try to make up her mind if she wanted to ask now. She must have decided not because she gave me the keys and got out of my way.

Judy said, "I need the wagon tonight, Dad, I got choir."

"Take the truck."

"I hate the truck. I don't like that stick shift."

"Just take the truck, all right?"

Now Judy was ready to start crying. I put the truck keys on the little table by the door and went out.

I was starving to death. I hadn't eaten anything since those two eggrolls before noon. I bought a hamburger and fries and a chocolate shake at Gaylord's there on Airport and ate them in the car. Then I got worried about Lane recognizing me, even in a different car. I looked around and found a bandanna in the back seat. I took off my tie and rolled up my shirt sleeves and put on my sunglasses. Then I tied the bandanna over my head, pirate style, the way I'd seen some biker guys do. Looked stupid as hell in the rear view mirror, but at least it didn't look much like me.

I made a pass all the way around the apartments and then parked out of sight of Lane's window. No sign of the Trans Am. The lights had been on behind her mini-blinds when I drove by. It was seven-thirty and full dark. A little after eight my bladder started to kill me.

I got out and peed against the back of the apartments, which didn't have any windows. From the smell there I wasn't the first.

A little after nine it started to rain.

By ten I thought maybe I'd made a mistake. That old Pinto wagon is too small for me and the springs in the seats are shot. I hurt like hell after ten minutes, let alone two and a half hours. I could have been in bed asleep. Worse yet, Javier could have showed up without me seeing him, or in another car.

I got out and walked up and down the parking lot. No Trans Ams. Lights still on in Lane's apartment. The rain soaked my bandanna and got in my shoes. Half an hour, I thought. Then I either go home or I go upstairs for a look. I was about to get back in the wagon when a black Trans Am pulled into the lot.

I ducked down and listened. The engine revved, then stopped. I could hear the hot metal tick and the rain make a softer tick against the hood. The door opened, the springs groaned, feet scraped against the asphalt. The door shut again. Silence. What if he can see me? My gun was still inside the Pinto.

I heard his footsteps move away. I could see his black leather coat as he went in the gate, Javier for sure, headed for the stairs. I waited until he was blocked by the corner of the apartment and then I crawled in the wagon head first. I stuck the little Colt in the back of my pants and jogged over to the other set of stairs, putting the jacket on as I ran.

By the time I got to the corner of the building, Lane had her door open. I heard her say, "There you are."

"You look nervous." Javier's voice. "Something wrong?"

"What do you think, you fucking prick? I'm going to welcome you with open arms?" I couldn't get used to the language she used. It just didn't fit with the way she looked.

"It's like raining out here, okay? Are you going to let me in, or what?"

"Yeah, I'm going to let you in."

A second later I heard the the door close. The locks went again and then there was a crash and a muffled shout and then silence.

I COULDN'T just stand there. Even if it was none of my business, even if I was carrying a gun I had no permit for, even if somebody in that apartment had trashed my truck and left me threatening notes.

I turned the corner and tried to see through the blinds. Nothing. I heard voices but I couldn't tell male or female, let alone what they were saying.

Christ Jesus. It's happening right now, and I can't let it go on.

I knocked on the door. It went so quiet in there I could hear the raindrops ping on the railing behind me. I stepped back and kept my hands away from my sides, away from the gun stuck down the back of my pants. I don't know how long I waited but it felt like at least a minute.

Something moved behind the peephole and the door opened on the chain. It was Lane, fully dressed, not a mark on her. I suddenly realized I was still wearing the bandanna and sunglasses. She laughed and it sounded more nervous than anything. I wadded up the glasses and bandanna in my left hand.

"Just go away," she said. "Don't pull any knight-in-shining-armor numbers, don't give me any shit, just go away. Tell your lawyer friend it's over. I'm dropping the charges. The law sucks, you can tell him that too. Happy now? Go fuck yourself and stay away."

She started to close the door. I stuck my foot in, I don't know why. I couldn't let it end that way.

"Look," I said, "I just want to say—"

"I don't want to hear it." She leaned on the door, and it hurt.

To hell with it. "Let me get my foot out and I'm gone," I said.

She eased off on the door and right then something crashed in the back of the apartment and I heard Javier's voice, muffled, yelling.

"Oh shit," Lane said. She took a step back.

A woman's voice from off to the side said, "Bring him in."

All of a sudden Lane's apartment didn't seem like such a good idea. The door slammed and I heard the chain come off and I turned around and ran for the stairs. Something hit me in the back of the knees and I skidded into the railing at the edge of the walkway. Then something metal poked me in the ear and a woman's voice said, "Get up and go inside."

My knees hurt where I'd slid. I got up real slow and the woman got behind me where I still couldn't see her. I walked back to the apartment. I was so scared that everything looked tilted and the light hurt my eyes. Then I was inside and she pushed me and I went down on my knees again, next to the far wall of the living room.

"Put your hands on your head," the woman said, "and turn around and sit against the wall." I did what she said. There was the gun still stuck down the back of my pants. All I wanted was out of there. If I could get the gun out without getting shot in the process, maybe I could walk away.

Lane was there, and two women I didn't know. The one with the gun was close to six feet tall, heavy, with crewcut blonde hair. She wore jeans and a plain white sweatshirt and a green flannel shirt over that. The sleeves of the flannel shirt were rolled up to show the sweatshirt underneath. The gun was some kind of little automatic and there was a silencer screwed on to the end of the barrel. That was when I realized for the first time that I was probably going to die.

The other woman was closer to my age. She had on jeans and a bulky orange sweater. Most of her hair had gone white. She had a pair of pliers which she was taking apart a plain wire coat hanger with. I could see a wad of paper on the breakfast bar that she'd torn off the hangar.

Against the wall across from me, behind the door, was Javier. They'd done something to his hair, cut a lot of it off the front, and it gave him a startled look. His hands were behind his back. One of his shoes was off and the sock was gone. His mouth was taped shut with silver duct tape. It looked like there was something in his mouth behind the tape. They'd run the tape all the way around his head a couple of times. I figured out where the missing sock was and decided I would be quiet.

"You know him?" the one with the gun said to Lane.

"He works for Asshole's lawyer. He's the one with the truck you fixed this afternoon. He's nobody, just hired meat."

"Scum," she said sadly. "What would make somebody take a job like that?"

"Money," the woman with the coat hanger said. "It's all about money. Even Asshole there, women are just property to him. Right, Asshole? Like cattle or something. You can do anything you want to them."

That was when I finally got it. "He's the one," I said.

The woman with the gun gave me a funny look. "I think Dr. Watson over here just figured something out."

"Javier," I said. "He's the one that…"

"Raped me," Lane said. "That's right. He raped me. Do you mean to sit there and tell me you didn't know?"

"I didn't know. But…I saw him here the other night. You called him by name…"

"Jesus," said the woman with the coat hanger. She sounded disgusted.

"Yeah, I know his name," Lane said. "I knew him before he raped me. So what? Because I know who he is, does that give him the right? I bought some coke from him, okay? And now my lawyer says he'll probably get off because of it. Even though he raped me. You want to hear about it? He pulled a knife, and he cut my clothes off, and he made me lie on my stomach, and he fucked me up the ass." She took two steps and kicked Javier in the face. She was wearing boots and she caught him on the cheekbone.

The woman with the coat hanger said, "Careful. Break his nose and he'll suffocate."

The woman with the gun said, "That'd be a real pity."

"Kind of misses the point, doesn't it? If we just *kill* him?" She had the hangar straightened out now and she was twisting one end into loops. It looked like a letter at the end of the straight piece of wire. It was a letter. It was the letter R.

"What are you going to do?" I said. Nobody paid any attention to me.

The woman with the coat hangar took it into the kitchen. I could see her through the breakfast bar. She took an ice bucket out of the freezer and set it on the counter. Then she bent the long end of the hangar double to make a handle. Then she got down a potholder, it was a red potholder, quilted in little diamond shapes, it fit over her hand like a mitten. Then she turned on a gas burner, turned it up to high. The flames were blue and the potholder was red.

Suddenly Javier started to spasm and make choking noises. There was a sour smell and he snorted a fine spray of vomit onto his clothes.

The woman with the coat hangar put it down on the stove and hurried over to take his gag off. The woman with the gun knelt on his legs and shoved the silencer into his crotch. "Don't make a sound," she told him. "Or you'll never fuck anybody again."

They were all looking at Javier. I got the Colt out. I was shaking again. It seemed like it was a million degrees below zero in that apartment. Javier spit puke on the floor and Lane ran into the kitchen for paper towels. She ran right past me and didn't even see the gun in my hand.

I stood up and the woman with the gun turned around. "What do you think you're—" She saw the Colt. Her face didn't change hardly at all. "So you want to play cowboy."

"I just want out of here. Let me walk out the door and you'll never see me again."

"I'd rather kill you," she said. I could tell she meant it. "I don't do anything with a gun pointed at me. So you can either use it or you can put it away."

We stayed like that, just looking at each other, pointing our guns at each other, Javier on his side, gasping, Lane with a handful of wet paper towels, the woman in the orange sweater standing to one side with a look on her face like she was only mildly interested. I tried to imagine myself pulling the trigger and knew I couldn't do it. It was the first rule my daddy taught me, that you don't pull a gun unless you're willing to use it, and here I'd gotten it wrong. I wondered how much noise her gun would make, with the silencer and all. I wondered if it would hurt.

"That's better," the woman with the gun said. I looked at my hand, saw my daddy's Colt now pointed down at the floor. My legs had gone weak and I eased down onto my knees and put the Colt on the cheap brown carpet between us.

I said, "Now what?"

The woman with the gun said, "Good question."

The woman in the sweater taped Javier's mouth shut again and went back in the kitchen. Lane went over to Javier and wiped up the mess on the floor. Then she got up and opened the front door.

The woman with the gun said, "Are you crazy?"

Lane looked at me, crooked her finger toward the door. "Get out of here."

The woman with the gun said, "Lane—"

"Let him go," Lane said. "Maybe he learned something."

I stood up. It didn't look like the woman with the gun was going to stop me. I took one careful step toward the door, and looked back. The woman with the coat hanger was holding it over the burner. A bright yellow flame was coming off it and the metal was turning red hot. I took another step and then I was walking, fast, and then I was outside and the door slammed shut behind me. I ran for the stairs and I was just to the corner of the building when I heard Javier, right through the tape, let out one long, muffled scream.

I JUST WANTED to finish it. I stopped at the Diamond Shamrock on Airport and called Dennis' house. The rain was still falling, slower now, and I turned up the collar of my jacket while I listened to the phone ring. His wife answered and told me he was at the office. I remembered he'd told me that.

I parked next to his Mercedes in the lot. I had to knock on the glass door of his office for him to come unlock it. He was working at the copier and there was a big stack of what looked like tax forms on the table next to it.

"What's up?" he said. He fed another form into the machine.

"Lane Rochelle's dropping the case," I said.

"You're kidding."

"That's what you wanted, isn't it? I mean, that's why you'd hire a big, stupid guy like me in the first place, right?"

"Maybe you're not so dumb as you look."

"Maybe not."

"I think this calls for a bonus. I expect my client could afford a couple hundred on top of your hourlies."

I expected it was worth a lot more than that to Dennis, not to have to put Javier on the stand, not to have him talk about his cocaine customers. But all I said was, "Why don't I get that bank bag for you?"

"Sure. It's in the desk there."

I went into Dennis' office and got the bank bag out of the side drawer. I guess I was just looking for something. I didn't know what it was going to be until I found it. I looked back into the waiting room and Dennis still had his back to me, feeding papers into the machine. I eased open the top drawer and there it was, a fat plastic bag full of cocaine. I figured it must have been about a quarter of a pound. I flattened it out and put it down the front of my pants and tucked my shirt back in around it.

I took the bank bag in to Dennis and he counted out three brand new hundred dollar bills. "Not bad for a day's work, eh?" he said. I couldn't do anything but nod. "You did good," he said. "There's plenty more where this came from. Just let me know, okay?"

I even shook his hand.

I went downstairs and jimmied the lock on the gas tank of his Mercedes. Then I took off the gas cap and poured the entire baggie of cocaine inside. When I closed it all back up I could hardly tell the difference. Then I threw the baggie in the dumpster. I don't really know what cocaine does to an engine, but I figure there's at least a lot of sugar in whatever it's cut with. Any way you look at it, it's just bound to be expensive.

I was still kind of pumped up when I got in the Pinto, but it wasn't like I thought it would be. I didn't feel any better. In fact I felt worse, I felt like hell. Lane said maybe I learned something, but if I did then maybe I learned the wrong thing. I got turned around and headed north on the I-35 access road, and I must not have been paying attention, because when I went to get on the freeway there was suddenly this car behind me that I never saw, his tires screaming on the wet road. I kept waiting for the thump as he hit me and it didn't happen, there was just his horn as he whipped around, leaning over in his seat to shake his fist at me. And there was nothing I could do except sit there and hold onto the wheel. Because there are all these millions of gestures for being pissed off and not one to say I'm sorry.

FLAGSTAFF

IT WAS NOT yet noon when they pulled into the motel. Rain in the early morning had rinsed the air and left it fresh and cool, tasting of the fall to come. Lee's father set the handbrake but left the engine running as he got out, boots crunching in the gravel.

Lee crawled halfway over the front seat to look at the dashboard clock. He crossed the fingers on both hands, daring to hope that the day's driving was already over, that they would not have to try motel after motel. Lee had a good feeling about this one. Its wooden siding was the color of milk chocolate, and the air through his open window tickled his nose with the green scent of pines and junipers. There was even a pool, though in truth it was too cold to think about swimming.

A white-haired lady opened cabin seven for Lee's father, and a few seconds later Lee heard a toilet flush, followed by a repeated clacking as his father tested the lock on the front door. Finally he came out nodding and then stood for a moment in the watery sunshine, long-sleeved khaki shirt buttoned to the throat, hands in the pockets of his pleated trousers, looking into the distance.

Lee tried to smile at his mother, who seemed oblivious.

They locked their suitcases in the room and drove back into town. Lee's father was whistling now, his right arm up on the seat back, his left elbow propped in the window, as if he were another man entirely from the one who'd been driving with fierce concentration since dawn. "So," he said to Lee's mother, "what do you think? Nice place, huh?"

She smiled bravely. "Very nice."

"There's a Rexall," Lee said. "With a fountain. Can we? Can we?"
His father sighed. "I suppose so."

They parked and Lee ran ahead. Hand-lettered signs in the drug store window advertised typing taper, Alka-Seltzer, cold cream. The sweet smell of frying meat hung in the air inside. Lee spun himself around and around on his chrome and red vinyl stool while his father read the menu. "Stop that," his father said, and Lee faced the counter, sitting on his hands to help himself keep still. When it was his turn Lee ordered a hamburger and a chocolate milkshake and then asked, "Can I look around?"

His father seemed to be studying himself in the long mirror behind the fountain. "Go," he said.

On a wire spin rack Lee found a Jules Verne he'd never seen before, a movie tie-in edition of *Master of the World* with Vincent Price on the cover. He stashed the book behind a stack of *Moonrakers* and moved on to the toy aisle. The cramped space was filled with Duncan yo-yos, Whammo Slip'N'Slides, and Mattel cap pistols. On the bottom shelf Lee found a Wiffle Ball and orange plastic bat that filled him with a longing he thought might overwhelm him.

He went back to the lunch counter and wolfed his food, then sat with his arms wrapped around his narrow chest, trying to gauge his father's mood while struggling with his own impatience, hope, and fear. His father ate slowly, drank a second cup of coffee, and smoked a cigarette while Lee's mother applied a fresh coat of lipstick. Finally Lee's father stood up with the check and started for the register by the front door. Lee tugged at his father's pants leg and showed him the book. His father glanced at it and nodded. "Okay."

He seemed distracted in a mild, pleasant way, so Lee pressed his advantage. "Look," he said, and showed his father the bat and ball.

"I thought you wanted the book."

He didn't seem angry so Lee said, "Can I have this and the book too?"

"What would you do with it? If I get this job, I'm not going to have time to play with you." Lee knew his father wouldn't have time to play with him in any case, but he was caught by something in his father's voice. His father was thinking about the job in the same way that Lee was thinking about the bat and ball. And though Lee knew,

even at ten years old, that the job would not work out, the hope
itself was contagious.

"Please?" he said.

In the car Lee's father said, "Roger Maris back there is going to
teach himself baseball and become a sports hero and the envy of all
his friends. If he had any."

The bat and ball were attached with wire to a long red piece of
cardboard that read "Junior Slugger." It made Lee happy to just to
hold it in his lap—the newness of it, the hard perfection of the plastic.
The possibilities.

They got back to the motel with the entire afternoon still in
front of them. Lee begged his father to play with him and eventually
his father relented. They stood under the sharp-smelling trees and
Lee swung at three pitches and missed them all, having to chase the
ball after each one. "Not so hard!" he said.

His father, cigarette in the corner of his mouth, grunted and
tossed him an easy, underhanded pitch. Lee connected and the ball
sailed past his father's outstretched hand, through the trees, to land
near the swimming pool.

"Don't look at *me*," his father said.

Lee ran after it, and by the time he got back his father was gone.

Lee tried to toss the ball up with one hand and hit it as it
dropped. It was harder than it looked, and after a while he went
back inside.

His father was teaching his mother a game he'd just learned. He
had five small dice that he kept in a prescription vial. It was like
poker, he told her, and he showed her how to draw up a score sheet
on a piece of scratch paper.

Lee's bed smelled like clean ironing, and he made a pile of pillows
to lean against while he read. His new book was about a man named
Robur who was brilliant but had no use for the world. He built a
flying platform and circled the earth in it, refusing to come down.
As he read, Lee was distantly aware of the patter of the dice and his
mother's nervous laughter.

Finally Lee's father said to him, "Why don't you get your nose
out of that goddamned book and go outside for a while?"

As Lee closed the door, carrying his new bat and ball, he heard the lock turn behind him. Ahead of him was the new city and the rest of the world.

He sat for a while in a green wooden chair at the edge of the swimming pool. The water had the pale color of a hot summer day, while the sky was a deep, artificial blue, the color of swimming pools and plastic cars. It was like the world was upside down.

Nearly four decades later, with a happy marriage, an elegant North Carolina home, a secure job, Lee has everything his father always dreamed of. But somehow one day has become like the next. That afternoon in Flagstaff haunts him, and the thing he least understands is how his memory of it could be suffused with such a quiet glow of happiness.

And in 1961 Lee raises the plastic bat to his shoulder, tosses the ball high above his head once more, and swings.

THE TALE OF
MARK THE BUNNY

ONE SPRING it stopped raining in early March and didn't start again.

There was one very well-off bunny in the village who had a large burrow and lots of food saved up. He wasn't worried about the drought at all. The other bunnies, though, looked at the purple-red nettles withering in the fields and the mayweed that hadn't even flowered and wondered if they were going to have enough food to get them through the next winter.

The very well-off bunny was named Albertus, but everybody called him Big Al—at least they called him that when they were sure he couldn't hear them. Big Al was in fact a very large bunny with long, white, silky fur. He had lots of land that his parents had left to him, and he never let any of the other bunnies gather food there. The story was that Big Al had sat on the one bunny who tried to make off with some of his carrots until the small bunny begged for mercy. After Big Al let him up, the small bunny moved to another village.

ONE MORNING a dozen or more bunnies sat around the village square, licking the dew off the dried and wrinkled clover to quench their thirsts, and talking about the drought. There was still a bit of a cool breeze from Possum Creek, a mile or so away. Sophie Bunny, who was large and sleek, with a black circle around one eye, was there with her husband Lenny and their youngest, Ralph, who still lived at home with them.

"I don't mind telling you," Lenny said, "I'm getting a little scared by all this." Lenny was a small, tan bunny with buck teeth and big cheeks like a chipmunk.

"No need to be afraid," said the short, overweight Reverend Billy Bunny, the village's spiritual leader. "The Easter Bunny will provide." He sat, as he usually did, by the thick green hawthorn bush in the middle of the square—although the bush was neither as thick nor as green as it had once been.

"Easter was two weeks ago," said Maria Bunny. "And there's not a cloud in the sky."

"I thought the Easter Bunny just did eggs," little Ralph said.

"Actually," Lenny said, "so did I."

"I never really understood what a bunny was doing with eggs in the first place," Sophie said, "if you want to know the truth."

"We could ask Big Al for help," Annie Bunny suggested. "He's got enough food for everybody."

It was well known that Big Al provided the Reverend Billy's food. He'd discovered Billy preaching in the village square a few years before and liked the fact that most of Billy's sermons were about keeping things the way they already were. Since then word had gone around that Big Al thought the other bunnies should pay attention when the Reverend Billy had something to say, and that he would frown on anyone who made fun of him in public. If anybody could talk to Big Al, it had to be the Reverend Billy.

"Well, ah, ahem," Billy said. Ever since he became official, he'd started to talk like a much older rabbit. "I think we should remember that the Easter Bunny helps those who help themselves." This was exactly the sort of thinking that had impressed Big Al.

"I agree," Annie said. "Let's help ourselves to some of Big Al's food."

Annie's husband Jonathan said, "I don't think that's what he meant."

Suddenly a bunny no one had ever seen before hopped out from behind a tree. He was very thin, with black fur and dark, intense eyes. "I know one thing you could do," he said. "You could stop eating all that clover while you're worrying about starving to death."

"Darn it!" Lenny said. "I *am* eating again."

"Who are you?" the Reverend Billy asked the stranger.

"My name is Mark."

Billy narrowed his eyes. "Are you the same Mark Bunny that used to live down by Clearwater Pond? The one that got kicked out of the village for being a troublemaker?"

"I guess I am," Mark said.

"Uh oh," somebody said. For a few seconds all the bunnies hopped around nervously, and when everyone quieted down again Mark had lots of space around him in all directions.

Billy continued to stare at Mark from his high position. "You keep moving along," he said. "We don't want your kind around here."

Mark looked at the other bunnies to see if anyone else wanted to speak up. When no one did he said, "Okay," and hopped slowly away.

LATE THAT AFTERNOON, as Sophie, Lenny, and Ralph headed home to their burrow, they saw Mark in the grass by the side of the path ahead of them.

"Oh dear," Lenny said. "It's that Mark bunny."

"I don't think he'd actually hurt us, do you?" Ralph said. "He just looks kind of sad."

"I don't know," Lenny said. "I'm afraid."

"I'm afraid too," Sophie said. "We're bunnies. We're always afraid. But sometimes we have to do the right thing, even when it's scary."

"And what exactly are you saying, in this case, the right thing might be?" Lenny asked.

"There's wolves around this time of year. We can't let him wander around all night without a burrow to stay in."

"Actually we could, if we wanted to…"

"Lenny…"

"Okay, okay, I'll go ask him."

Lenny hopped carefully over toward Mark. "Um, hi," Lenny said. Mark nodded.

"My wife," Lenny said, "er, that is, *we,* wanted to know if maybe you needed a place to stay tonight? Of course if you have someplace else, that would be perfectly fine and we wouldn't feel in the least insulted if you turned us down."

"No, Mark said, "I don't have a place. That's very kind of you."

"We've got some strawberries we've been saving," little Ralph said, bounding up. "They're kind of small, but you could have one."

"I do love strawberries," Mark said. "But you'll have to let me do something for you in return."

"How come?" Ralph said.

"That's just my philosophy."

"What's a philosophy?"

"Well," Mark said, "I guess it's just some ideas about life."

"Oh. Why don't you just say 'ideas about life,' then?"

"Ralph," Sophie said, "you're being rude."

"Sorry," Ralph said.

That evening, after sharing the strawberries, the four bunnies lay happily on the floor of the burrow. "Tell me some more about this philosophy of yours," Sophie said. Sophie was always interested in new things.

"You mean my ideas about life?" Mark asked. Ralph laughed at that and Mark wiggled his whiskers and went on. "Really I just have this one idea. I've thought about it a lot and got it down to the simplest words I could."

"So what is it?" Lenny asked.

Mark sat up and spoke in a deep voice, clearly liking the sound of the words as they came out. "'Give what you can. Take what you need.'"

"Is that what got you in trouble at Clearwater Pond?" Sophie asked.

"Actually most people seemed to like my idea, once they thought about it. There was just this one very well-off bunny named Sophocles who got upset, and told everybody I was dangerous."

"Are all rich bunnies mean?" Ralph asked.

"I've traveled around quite a bit," Mark said, "and I've seen rich bunnies who were very kind and generous. I've also seen quite a few who did tend to be a bit selfish."

"So are you saying," Sophie asked, "that if we get hungry enough it's okay to take some of Big Al's food?"

"Only if Big Al had already given up what he could for you to take from. Everybody has to agree. That's the hard part, of course, for those that have more than enough to give some of it up."

"It's hard to think about," Lenny said. "It scares me."

"Bunnies are always afraid," Sophie said. "But sometimes…"

"I know," Lenny said. "I know." He thought for a while. "Do you think if all of us put all our food together—except for Big Al, of course—we'd have enough to get us through the drought?"

"I don't think so," Sophie said.

Mark shrugged his shoulders and lay down again. "That's where the luck part comes in."

MARK LEFT before the others got up the next morning. When little Ralph went outside he found something very strange and called for his parents to come look. It seemed Mark had chewed some of the leaves off a nearby hawthorn bush and stuck some new branches where there hadn't been any before. Sophie, Lenny, and Ralph all looked at it for a while.

"You know," Lenny said, "it almost looks like…nah. Couldn't be."

"Looks like what?" Sophie said. She was finishing her morning grooming, licking her front paws and then rubbing them over her big, silky ears.

"Well, except for being green and everything, don't you think it looks a bit like Ralph?"

"I think it looks a lot like Ralph," Sophie said.

"Why would somebody make a tree look like a bunny?" Lenny asked.

"I think it's called 'art,'" Sophie said.

"'Art,'" Lenny said. "No doubt about it. That was one weird bunny."

"I liked him," Ralph said.

"Me, too," said Sophie."

"I don't know," Lenny said. "I lay awake for a long time last night thinking about his—" He looked at Ralph. "—ideas about life, and this morning my head hurts. Now I look at this 'art' thing and it makes my head hurt too." Slowly he reached up with his rear leg to scratch under his chin. "Okay," he said, "maybe it hurts in a nice kind of way."

THEY ALL WENT back to the village that morning to talk some more about the drought. Everyone seemed a little crankier and a little thirstier than the day before.

"Everyone should just eat less," the Reverend Billy said.

"Some of us aren't eating much at all right *now*," Maria said. She was in fact a very thin bunny, going gray in many places.

There was a long silence.

"What if we…" Lenny swallowed hard. "What if everybody gave all they could and only took what they needed?"

All the other bunnies turned to look at him. "What?" Jonathan asked.

The Reverend Billy hopped over from the high place in the middle of the square and stared right into Lenny's eyes. "What are you?" he said, squinting. "Some kind of Markist?"

Lenny took a short hop backwards without really meaning to.

"That's not very nice," Sophie said.

"That sounds like name-calling," said little Ralphie.

"I'm only speaking the truth," said the Reverend.

"It might be only speaking the truth to say somebody was short and fat," said Sophie, "but it still wouldn't be very nice to say it in that tone of voice."

The Reverend Billy, who was in fact rather short and fat, wrinkled up his nose and said, "Hmmph."

"Look," Sophie said. "The problem is water, right? But there's all the water we would ever need over in Possum Creek."

"What are you saying, that we should move the village?" Jonathan asked. "I don't like it by the creek, with all those holly bushes. Besides, wolves live there. And it would take forever to make new burrows."

"No," Sophie said, "I wasn't thinking about moving the village. I was thinking—what if we made the water come to us?"

APPARENTLY SOPHIE had been awake much of the night thinking, too. She knew that Possum Creek had once flowed right by the village, many, many years before Sophie's mother had been born. It had filled up with sand and after that the river had flowed away to other places.

But if there was one thing bunnies were good at, besides eating and having big families, it was digging. What if they dug out the old river bed and made part of Possum Creek—just a small part, not enough to hurt anyone downstream—come through their village again? Then after it came through the village it could go back and join back up with the main river.

After Sophie finished talking about her plan, the other bunnies found that their heads hurt just as much as Lenny's did. They all started to talk at once and it was almost an hour before it got quiet enough for Lenny to speak up.

"I've heard what everybody has to say," he said, "which mostly seems to be that they're afraid. Well, I can understand that. But we have to do something, or we won't have any food. I think everybody who wants to give what they can to this plan should meet us tomorrow down at Possum Creek."

LENNY AND SOPHIE and Ralph all slept badly that night, but as soon as the first rays of sunshine trickled into their burrow they got up and went to Possum Creek. By the time the sun was fully up there were only five other bunnies there.

"Thank you all for coming," Lenny said, and looked up at the sky. "Boy, it looks like it's going to be another really hot day."

It looked like he shouldn't have said that, because as soon as he did, Jonathan made a little hop like he was going to try to sneak away.

"Good thing we're here by the *river*, then, isn't it?" said Sophie in a funny voice. "Where it's so *cool* and *nice?*"

"Uh, yeah!" Lenny said. "Sure is!"

"Right, Jonathan?" Sophie said.

Jonathan saw that all the bunnies were now looking at him. "I guess so," he said.

Sophie showed them what she'd been thinking, which was to start digging inland a little way from the river bank. That would leave a wall of dirt between the river and the ditch they were going to dig, so no water would get in the hole. Then, when they were all done, they could dig through the wall and let the water in.

"I figure we should start digging about here," Sophie said, scratching a line in the dirt with one paw.

"Well," Lenny said, "what are we waiting for? Let's make a river!"

They dug all day, and when they were done their paws were sore and their legs were tired, but they had a wide, deep channel about fifty feet long. In the last of the daylight they stood looking at it.

"This isn't going to work," Sophie said, very quietly, so nobody but Lenny could hear her. "It's just too much work and there aren't enough of us."

"It was a good idea, though," Lenny said.

"And you did your best," Sophie said. "You worked harder than anyone."

"So what happens now?"

"I don't know," Sophie said. "I'm all out of ideas."

Just then Jonathan started to hop slowly along the edges of the hole, looking at what they'd done. He seemed to be thinking very hard.

"This is it," Sophie whispered. "When Jonathan gives up, the others will, too."

Jonathan stopped and turned to face the other bunnies. He sat up on his hind legs and said, "Look! Look what we did!"

"It's not so bad," Lenny said.

"Not so bad?" Jonathan said. "Not so bad? It's *wonderful*. We're only bunnies, and we did this. We made this great big hole, which isn't just a hole, it's the start of a new river. Instead of just sitting around and being scared and hungry, we did something about it! I'm going to tell *everybody!*"

THE NEXT MORNING there were forty eager bunnies at the trench, and still more showed up as the day went on. Sophie and Lenny had to stop frequently to answer questions and explain Sophie's idea over and over. But with forty bunnies digging and laughing and having fun, the work went much faster than it had the day before.

In the afternoon Jane Bunny came to the edge of the ditch and asked if she could talk to Sophie. Sophie hopped out and said, "What can I do for you?"

"No, it's me," Jane said. "I want to do something for *you*. But I can't dig." She held up her left front leg, which had never worked right, even when she was a baby.

"There is something you can do," Sophie said. "If you really want to."

Sophie explained her ideas to Jane, who actually had some ideas of her own. For instance, she thought of making trees that had grown up in the old riverbed into islands, so the bunnies wouldn't have to dig them up or move to higher ground to get around them. Jane was able to hop up and down along the trench and answer questions and carry messages back and forth between the other workers.

On the third day, even more bunnies showed up. One of them was Albertus, though he hadn't come to work. He sat on a hill and watched for long enough that everyone could see him, and see that he was unhappy, before he hopped slowly away.

THAT EVENING the Reverend Billy Bunny called a meeting in the village square. "What you're doing," he said, "just isn't natural."

"Bunnies dig," Maria said. "What's unnatural about that?"

"You're changing things," the Reverend Billy said.

"We're just putting the river back where it used to be," Jane said. "We're not hurting any other animals."

"Only the Easter Bunny," the Reverend Billy said, "is supposed to change the shape of the land."

This was a very difficult idea and everyone got very quiet to think about it. It was a hot night, with stars almost as bright as the Moon, and crickets sang all around them.

Suddenly a voice spoke up from the back of the crowd.

"Eggs," little Ralph said.

The Reverend Billy seemed startled. "What did you say?"

"I said, 'eggs,'" Ralph told him. "I thought the Easter Bunny was just in charge of Easter eggs."

"Well, er, um..."

"Yeah," said Lenny, who seemed to be much less afraid than he used to be. "Who said the Easter bunny was in charge of rivers?"

"Yeah," said Annie. "You're always telling us the Easter Bunny helps those who help themselves. If this isn't helping ourselves, what is?"

"But, er, well..."

The bunnies, one and two at a time, began to slowly hop away from the square. "We're tired," Jonathan said as he left. "Let's do this some other time."

"If you want to help us dig," Maria said, "we'd be happy to see you tomorrow."

THE REVEREND Billy Bunny didn't show up to dig the next day, or any of the days after. However, he didn't call any more meetings either, which many of the bunnies thought almost made up for his not working.

Soon the hole went right up to the edge of the village. Some of the bunnies wanted to quit right then and there and let the water into the ditch, but Jane spoke up. "You've seen how water gets bad if it doesn't keep moving. We need to finish the job, just like Sophie said."

Other bunnies had ideas, too. Little Ralph surprised even himself when he figured out that they needed to tunnel under a big tree that had fallen across the old riverbed instead of going around it or trying to move it. "That way," he said, "when the water goes under it, we can use it to get to the other side."

Three weeks from the day they first broke ground, the ditch was almost finished. Sophie and Lenny together broke through at the downstream end, where the little river would eventually join back with the big one. All that was left was to break through the wall at the upstream end and let the water in.

THE ENTIRE VILLAGE gathered at the river, ready to celebrate, including old Albertus, who had found another hill where he could look down on them. Even the Reverend Billy was there, trying to look stern and disapproving.

Though there still hadn't been any rain in the bunnies' village, it had been raining upstream. The river was full of water and running very, very fast.

"You know," Sophie said, "We could have a problem here."

"What do you mean?" Lenny asked. "C'mon, c'mon, we've been working on this forever. Bunnies aren't very patient, you know. Let's finish this!"

"I'm afraid—"

"Bunnies are always afraid," Lenny said. "But sometimes—"

"No," Sophie said. "This is different. When we dig through that last wall of dirt, the whole river is going to rush right into our new hole. Whoever does it could get really, really hurt."

"Oh," Lenny said. "Do you think?"

They all stood and looked at the river, which no longer seemed peaceful, but seemed a little angry. Then they looked at Sophie's ditch. Then they looked at the river again.

"I'll do it," Lenny said.

"Lenny, no," Sophie said. "I won't let you."

"Somebody's got to do it," Lenny said. "It might as well be me."

"No," said a deep voice behind them. "It has to be me."

They all turned. "You?" Lenny said.

"Me," Albertus said.

"But…but…that doesn't make any sense," Sophie said. "You're *rich*."

"I used to be," Albertus said.

The others gathered around to listen. "What happened?" Maria asked.

"Back in February, when I went down to look at all my lovely food, it was gone."

"Gone?" Jonathan said.

"Mice," Albertus said. "They tunneled into my vault, between the big rocks, and they took everything. And because my land is so high up, the drought hurt me worse than anyone else."

"Why didn't you tell us?" Sophie asked.

"Why didn't you tell *me*?" Reverend Billy asked. He seemed more upset than Albertus was.

"I know you don't like me," Albertus said. "I know what you all call me behind my back. 'Albert Doo-Doo head.'"

"Um, actually, nobody's ever called you that," Ralph said.

"Really?"

"Really. 'Big Al,' that's what everybody calls you."

"'Big Al' isn't so bad," Albertus said thoughtfully. "Anyway, I've been hearing all these ideas going around, all this, 'give what you can, take what you can get away with—'"

"'Take what you *need*,'" Lenny said. "There's a difference."

"Whatever. At first I thought I would come sit on one of you until you gave me some food. But none of you has any food either. That was when it hit me: I'm the same as anybody else now."

"Wow," Maria said.

"I'm not exactly happy about it," Albertus said. "I stayed in my burrow and sulked for a long time. But after a while I would come out here and watch all of you digging. It looked like fun, but I didn't know how to, well, to ask to join in."

"I guess you just did," Sophie said. "Frankly, I think you have a lot to make up for, but if I understand what Mark taught us, once you're willing to give what you can, you're in."

"Thank you," Albertus said. "I mean that."

"I hope you meant what you said about digging through to the river," Lenny said.

"I did," Albertus said, "and I do."

With that he hopped into the hole and began to dig. Soon his paws were damp and muddy, and very slowly water began to seep into the ditch.

"Oh my," Sophie said. "Oh my. This might actually work."

"Are you just now figuring that out?" Lenny said.

Albertus kept digging. Dirty water splashed his beautiful white coat until he was almost as brown as Lenny, and his powerful forepaws sent mud and rocks flying out of the hole.

Jonathan began to hop up and down in one place. "Look out!" he said. "Look out! It's coming!"

With a roar the water broke through the wall, and it swept Albertus away with it. The last they saw of him before he disappeared around a bend in the brand new river was one massive paw raised in farewell.

"OH NO!" Sophie cried, and she began to run after Albertus. So did all the other bunnies, but the new river was much, much faster than they were and they couldn't begin to catch up.

The bunnies, all of whom had been working very hard for many days, simply ran out of strength before they even got to the village. Sophie dropped to the ground panting, and Lenny fell down beside her.

"I didn't want this to happen," she said. "I was mad at him because he never wanted to share his food, but I didn't want this. It's all my fault."

"What's all your fault?" asked a deep voice.

All the bunnies looked up from where they were sprawled on the dry grass.

"Albertus!" Sophie said. "Are you all right?"

"Apparently someone left a tree across the new river," Albertus said. "I was able to hold on and pull myself out."

"That was little Ralph," Lenny said proudly.

Albertus nodded at him grandly. "Thank you, young bunny," he said. "If you wish, you may call me 'Big Al.'"

THE BUNNIES wanted to call it "Sophie's River," but Sophie said they should name it after Mark. They all nodded and pretended to agree with her, but went on calling it Sophie's River anyway.

The grass and the clover and the nettles began to bloom again almost immediately, and even the old hawthorn bush in the middle of the village square started to perk up. As soon as it did, though, a very strange thing happened. One night someone nibbled and worked at the bush until it came to look exactly like Mark the Bunny, whose ideas had inspired Sophie to save the village.

For several days afterwards Lenny had a bad stomach ache, and when anyone asked him if he'd made the art in the village square he would only say that the question made his head hurt.

CASTLES MADE OF SAND

JIM WORKED for a rental company—jackhammers, barricades, portable signs. He met Karla when he hired some temporaries from the agency she managed. There was just something about her. A sense that if anybody ever sprung her loose she might be capable of almost anything.

They got off to a slow start. She phoned just as he was leaving to pick her up for their first date. She was still at the office and would be there at least another hour. Could she come by and get him instead, late, maybe around nine?

Jim said okay. They had a slightly out-of-kilter dinner during which Karla drank too much wine and Jim too much coffee. When they got back to Jim's apartment, Jim asked her in, little more than a formality. She begged off because of an early meeting the next day. This is going nowhere, Jim thought. But when he leaned over to kiss her goodnight she met him with her mouth already open.

She was a little overweight, with permed hair somewhere between blonde and brown, almost no color at all. Jim's hair was black and thinning, and some mornings he felt like a toy whose stuffing was migrating out of the arms and legs and into the middle. He was in the final stages of his second divorce. Karla had been married once, briefly, right out of high school. That was now a while ago.

It wasn't like they were laughing all the time. Mostly they talked about things that happened at their jobs. None of that seemed important to Jim. What counted was that, from the first, he could see they needed something in each other.

Karla was in no particular rush to have sex. Still, after a few weeks, it was clearly only a matter of time. Jim carefully raised the subject one night as they lay on his couch, watching old sitcoms on Nickelodeon. Karla thought they should make a big deal out of it, go away for the weekend. Maybe down to Galveston.

The next day she called him at work. She'd just seen a thing in the paper about a sand castle contest at Surfside Beach that coming Saturday. "Sure," Jim said. "Why not?"

IT WAS A two hour drive to Surfside. Jim had been in a fender-bender midweek so they were in a rented Escort, courtesy of his insurance company. They got there around noon. They had to buy a beach parking permit, a little red sticker that cost six dollars and was good through the end of the year.

Jim was uncomfortable in baggy swim shorts and a T-shirt with a hole under one arm. He didn't want to put the sticker on a rent car and not get the rest of the use out of it.

"Maybe you can peel it off when you get home," Karla said.

"Maybe I can't."

"I'll pay for the sticker, how's that?"

"It's not the money, it's the principle."

Karla sighed and folded her arms and leaned back into the farthest corner of the front seat.

"Okay," Jim said. "Okay, for Christ's sake, I'm putting it on."

They turned left and drove down the beach. It was the first of June, indisputable summer. The sun blazed down on big cylinders of brown water that crashed and foamed right up to the edge of the road. The sand was a damp tan color and Jim worried about the car getting stuck, even though there was no sign of anyone else having trouble.

They drove for ten minutes with no sign of a sand castle. The beach was packed with red cars and little kids, college boys with coozie cups and white gimme caps, divorced mothers on green and yellow lawn chairs. Portable stereos played dance music cranked so high it sounded like no more than bursts of static. They drove under a pier with a sign that said, "Order Food Here," only there was no sign of food or anybody to give the order to. The air smelled of creosote and decay and hot sunlight.

Finally Jim saw a two-story blue frame building. A van from a soft-rock radio station was playing oldies at deafening volume and there were colored pennants on strings. It was not the mob scene Jim expected. He parked the Escort on a hard-packed stretch of sand and they got out. The sea air felt like a hot cotton compress. A drop of sweat broke loose and rolled down Jim's left side. He didn't know if he should reach for Karla's hand or not.

There were half a dozen sand sculptures inside the staked-out area. Jim looked up the beach and didn't see anything but more cars and coolers and lawn chairs. "I guess this is it?" he said. Karla shrugged.

At the far end was a life-size shark with a diver's head in its mouth. It had been spray-painted in black and gray and flesh tones, with a splatter of red around the shark's mouth. Next to it a guy and three women were digging a moat. They all had long hair and skimpy bathing suits.

Jim stepped over the rope that separated them. "Is this it?" he said to the guy, half-shouting over the noise from the van.

"There's the big contest over on Galveston. They got architects, you know. Kind of like the professionals, and we're just the amateurs."

"I thought there would be, I don't know. More."

"The Galveston contest is big. They got, like this giant ice cream cone with the earth spilling out of it, they got animals, they got a giant dollar bill made of sand. I mean, perfect."

Jim looked back at Karla, still on the other side of the rope, and then said, "You do this every year?"

"Nah, this is my first time. I thought, what the hey. It's free, anybody can do it. You should enter, you and the lady. They got buckets and shovels and stuff over to the van. Hell, they got twelve trophies and not near that many people. You're sure to win something. There's a good spot right here next to us." He pointed to a stake with an entry number on it, stuck in a flat piece of ground.

"I don't know."

"You should at least go look at the trophies."

Jim nodded and the guy went back to work. It was too early to tell what his was going to look like. Jim stepped back over the rope and he and Karla looked at the other entries. There was only one real castle, pretty nice, looking like it had grown out of the top of a low hill. There was a sea serpent with a long tail. The other two both seemed to be some kind of humanoid figures, slowly emerging from the sand.

"This is kind of a let down," Jim said.

"I wonder what they do with them after," Karla said. Jim could barely hear her over the music.

"What do you mean?"

"They're too high up for the tide to wash them out. That's what's supposed to happen, right? Digging moats and everybody running around, trying to delay the inevitable?"

Jim shook his head. "Want a Coke or something?"

"I don't know. Do you want to enter? Get a trophy?"

"I don't think so."

"Come on. It might be fun."

Jim looked at the flat patch of sand, the stake. He couldn't see it. "I'm going back to the car for a Coke. You want one or not?"

"I guess."

HE TOOK HIS TIME, trying to shake his mood. Nothing was ever easy. Everything was a struggle, and usually an argument besides. He unlocked the trunk and got two Cokes out of the ice, which was mostly melted already. He popped one and took a long drink, then started back.

He couldn't find Karla at first. He wandered around for a minute or so, then found her down near the water line. She'd taken a bucket and a garden trowel from the contest and built herself an elevated square of sand. On top of that she was dribbling watery mud from a bucket, making little twisty upside-down icicles. He watched her make five or six before she looked up.

She seemed to be blushing. "I used to do this when I was a kid," she said. "I called it the Enchanted Forest."

He squatted on his heels beside her.

She said, "You think this is really stupid, don't you." She took another handful of mud, made another tree.

"No," he said. He looked from the Enchanted Forest to the Gulf and back again. Close to shore the water was brown and foaming, farther out it was a deep shade of blue. He felt something inside him melting and collapsing and washing away.

"No," he said. "It's beautiful."